THE GIGGLERS

By Katy Charlotte Grubb

Illustrations by Lorna Grubb & Katy Charlotte Grubb

Based on 'The Gigglers' Screenplay
By Katy Charlotte Grubb

This book is dedicated to
Lorna Grubb.
My best friend and most trusted confidant.
The greatest mum in the whole world.

And also to Anita Hobbs.
Working with you has changed my life.
Thank you for everything.

All my love,

Katy xxx

THE GIGGLERS

1.

The college campus appeared to be deserted apart from a few security guards strolling about. Pushing up the sleeve of the vintage leather jacket, he glanced at his watch. 21:00.

Good. Bang on schedule.

Leaving the van parked around the corner, he had crept surreptitiously to the back of the dorm building. Now, he crouched behind the foliage, peering through a gap in the leaves. The hedge concealed his stocky frame while still allowing him an unobscured view of the ground floor window; the only one that was lit.

The blinds were up, and he could see the girl. Ashley. She was sat at her desk behind an open laptop, gabbing away on the phone. Teenybopper pop music blared through the half-open window.

⋈

"Oh my *god*," Ashley squealed. "Oh my god… I don't even wanna think about it right now… Oh my god. I'll call him tonight, I promise… Wait just one sec." Jemima — Ashley's tortoiseshell tabby, fed up

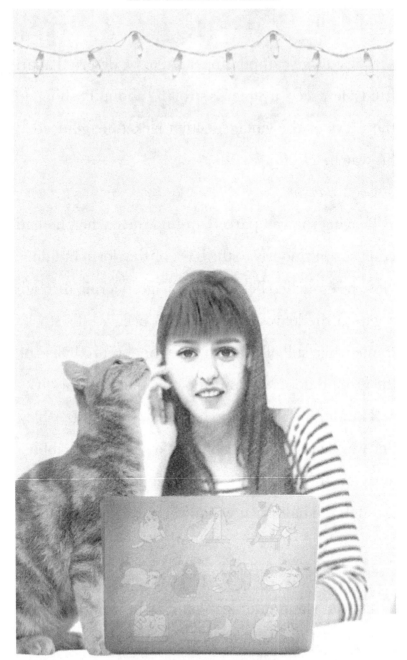

with having to compete for her attention, had plonked herself onto the keyboard, causing the music to stutter.

"Really, Jemima. Do you have to sit *right* there?" With an exaggerated sigh, Ashley scooped the cat up and placed her down on the floor. "Sorry. Jemima's being a pain." As if to show her umbrage at this remark, Jemima leapt back up. She began rubbing against the MacBook screen (covering it with hairs from her glossy coat), while simultaneously trying to head-butt the phone out of Ashley's hand. "No, I swear I will! I do too! Okay. Oh my god, *fine*. Just give me like an hour to zone out. I'm hanging up!"

Setting the phone down on the desk, Ashley now addressed Jemima, who had resumed her place in the middle of the keyboard. "*Jemima.* Cut it out!" At this, Jemima jumped down from the desk of her own accord and stalked off in a huff.

As Ashley began to dust the hairs off the screen with a Kleenex, a series of Facebook messages popped up from her best friend Carla:

'CALL BRIAN.'

'ASHHHH'

'Ash im sireous!'

'don't be a prude omg call him'

'im at the gym right now — tell me when youve talked to him k?'

Ashley quickly typed out a reply:

'OMG are you at the POOL right now? You're obsessed! K'babe, ttyl'

She was about to close the window when she saw a link to a new PopRush article had come up on her news-feed; 'The Gigglers: Where are they now?' She clicked on it and the page began to load.

Beneath the headline was a large flashy publicity shot of The Gigglers, as they had looked in the mid-2000s: Lolly, Roxie, Marky-Mark, Ricky and Polka-Dot Pete.

Ashley continued to scroll until she came to a slideshow.

ᴨ⧄

1 of 6.

"Lolly POPS UP uninvited at Teen Choice Awards!

Lauren DeWitt AKA Lolly crashed the glitzy award ceremony, coincidentally, during the Choice Hissy Fit announcement."

Underneath the headline was a picture of Lolly, as Ashley remembered her. Her dark curly hair fixed in a high ponytail, tied back with a pink floral scrunchie.

Next to this photo was a GIF. An image of Lolly, drunk and high, dressed in her Gigglers costume, throwing a drink on the floor and grimacing: 'YOUU GUYS LUV ME BUT WHATEVS!' Its two seconds were on a loop...

ᵖᵈ

2 of 6.

"Punter-Marky caught red-handed in Red Light Raid! Again! Does the former heartthrob have a lonely heart? Giggler Marky-Mark Rodriguez says he is 'not sorry, not even close.' "

There was a candid snap of Marky-Mark on the set of The Gigglers, and another of Marky on the cover of Teen Beat. The cover photo was instantly recognisable to Ashley, as that was the issue where they were giving

away that awesome Marky-Mark life-size poster.

Below were two mugshots. One of Marky-Mark, looking older and dishevelled (but still hot, Ashley thought), and one of this… Buena Buena.

><

3 of 6.

"Roxie & Lolly Sex Tape LEAKED! Download FULL VERSION HERE. TVNow's favourite giggling gals get a biology lesson! FOR THREE… Who's the lucky lad?"

Seeing Roxie and Lolly's names together made Ashley's stomach lurch.

She clicked on the blurry screenshot underneath and it came to life. It was Lolly and Roxie, she could see. And they were in a *ménage au trois* with a man. His face was hidden from the camera.

Ashley hurriedly clicked to the next slide.

><

4 of 6.

"Rude Ricky in Booze-fuelled Rage…

Richard Kilpatrick held in custody 'for aggravated

assault'. 22-year-old AmberLynn Daniels and 23-year-old Breanne Tackett recognised Mr. Kilpatrick outside The Borealis nightclub. Ms. Daniels took out her phone to snap a picture of the former child star. Enraged, Mr. Kilpatrick knocked her phone to the ground and stamped on it. When Ms. Tackett tried to intervene, he grabbed her by the hair, pulling out two hair extensions!"

There was Ricky, twinkling out in a press photo. Next to this polished publicity still was a mugshot with Ricky glaring morosely into the lens. Below, a video showed grainy CCTV footage of the frenzied attack.

⫘

5 of 6.

"Polka-Dot Pete Can Finally Ditch The Stripes.

After serving 7 months of his 13-month sentence for 2nd-degree arson, Peter Luderer is released for good behaviour. His publicist has not released a statement, but sources close to the former star insist that he has been rehabilitated."

The first picture showed Polka-Dot Pete in his

Gigglers costume; neon orange shirt with a green and white polka-dot bow tie and baggy polka-dot trousers to match. The second image showed a well-built young man in his late twenties. He was being arraigned in a striped jumpsuit.

❧

6 of 6.

The final slide read:

"TVNow Execs are not laughing. According to a statement by Glenn Ferrier at MediaOne, the producers of The Gigglers are 'shocked and disturbed by these events' and 'could have in no way anticipated' the actions of their stars.

When the show was abruptly yanked off the fall lineup back in 2010, there were stories circulating about the actors' behaviour onset. However, these rumours have never been confirmed by TVNow or MediaOne. Representatives at the network declined our repeated requests for comment.

None of the five disgraced actors could be reached at the time of publication."

ᴻ

Just then the power cut out, and Ashley gave a yelp; grabbing her phone, she scrambled onto the bed and adjusted the display brightness to halfway. There was only twenty percent left on the battery so Ashley set the phone to airplane mode; praying that the battery life would last until the electricity came back on.

As she aimed the light from the phone screen at different shadowy corners around the room, it got her thinking of the particle throwers in the Ghostbusters movies.

Years ago, at Suzy Henry's ninth birthday sleepover, Suzy's dad had bought Ghostbusters II for them from the Blockbuster clearance sale. The first Ghostbusters movie had been more funny than scary, but Ghostbusters II was (as Great Granny Turner used to say) a different kettle of fish. From the beginning when the pram with the baby rolled out into the road and nearly got hit by traffic, to the horrible bit where the pink slime came out of the bath tap. But the scariest, the most ultra-terrifying scene of the whole movie was when

the demonic nanny ghost zoomed through the sky, stretched out a super-long arm, and snatched the baby (who was held upright on the window ledge) while Sigourney Weaver's character looked on in horror.

Shivering at the memory, Ashley glanced over at the open window — and instantly wished she hadn't. She moved further into the middle of the bed and patted the duvet beside her. "Jemima," she called softly into the darkness. "Jemima, baby, I'm sorry I was grumpy. Jemima, please—"

A loud crash came from the bathroom.

"*Jemima?*"

Swinging her legs over the side of the bed, Ashley stood up. "*Jemima?!*"

Standing in the doorway of the bathroom, she directed the light down towards the floor. There was a sharp draught coming from the open (*broken?*) bathroom window. Then Ashley froze, as she suddenly became aware that there was someone else in the room; and as if reading her mind, the intruder chuckled. "Well, hey there, Ashley. How's it going?"

As she began to scream, he reached out and grabbed her; pulling her writhing body against his. Holding Ashley easily with one arm, he retrieved a stun gun and pressed it against the side of her neck.

2.

Stroke by stroke, Carla propelled herself through the water. It was twenty minutes before closing time and she was completing her final length of the evening.

She had joined the gym a few weeks after enrolling at college, and her evening swim sessions quickly became an essential part of her routine. Not only was the daily exercise vital to keep her body in good shape, but it also helped unclutter her mind. As she swam, all thoughts of lectures and work schedules seemed to disperse into a chlorinated haze.

Reaching the end, Carla climbed out and gave her hair a rough-dry with her towel. She placed it down and went to sit by the edge of the pool. By now the gym was empty and it was blissfully quiet. Dangling her feet in the water, she enjoyed the last few minutes of solitude. Carla gazed down at her reflection... and flinched.

Then she began to scream, as a pair of hands grabbed her from behind and pinned the towel over her face.

It had been dampened with some chemical substance. A sickly-sweet noxious odour that made Carla retch. For the first couple of seconds, she fought against inhaling the fumes. Then, taking a series of sharp involuntary breaths through her nose, her thrashing arms and legs gradually grew heavier until she slipped into unconsciousness.

⚔

It was ten-fifteen as Harry backed into his garage. After an interminably long client meeting, all he wanted was to put his feet up for the evening (what was left of it) in front of the television with a chilled glass of Prosecco. Harry checked his phone and noticed a series of missed calls. *Dad. He'd call him back tomorrow.* Putting the phone in his blazer pocket, he grabbed his briefcase from the footwell and shut the car door.

Standing in the driveway, Harry felt a distinct sense of unease as he tapped the code into the garage door keypad. There was something *off*, but he couldn't figure out what. It was then, as Harry watched the door slide down and the automatic light went off inside, that he

noticed the waft of cigarette smoke in the air.

Clutching the keys in a hammer grip, he went around the corner to the front of the house. Then he stopped still, as he saw there was a woman — an oddly familiar woman, standing on the porch. Her face was in shadow, but there was something about her stance that evoked a sense of *nostalgia* for him? No, that wasn't the word he was looking for. It was...

"Harry... Harry Ferrier?"

Harry nodded, and she stepped forward.

Suddenly the sound of running feet came charging up behind him, and before Harry had time to turn around, a sickening clunk to the back of the head knocked him out cold.

⚔

"Hey, Judy?" Will called to the pretty blonde working behind the bar. "Would you mind keeping an eye on our drinks? Tell Megan, when she gets back, that I've gone for a smoke." Judy nodded and Will made his way out of the packed bar.

Standing near one of the outdoor heaters, Will

fumbled around in his jacket pocket for his lighter and packet of Luckies. At that moment he spotted Amber with a crowd of her friends. He and Amber had had a thing some months back. They'd both been at this party during orientation week, then afterwards, pretty drunk, they had gone back to Amber's dorm and ended up sleeping together. Will had gotten up early the next morning and left without waking her.

They hadn't spoken since then; admittedly because he'd blocked her number. It wasn't as though he'd *planned* it that way, but when she started texting him later that day, what was supposed to have been just a casual thing started to feel way too messy, and he thought it was best just to cut contact.

Still, the last thing he wanted was for Megan to come out and find him in a drunken showdown with Amber and her friends. They didn't appear to have noticed him, so Will slinked off to the parking lot for his smoke. He was just about to take a puff when someone tapped him on the shoulder.

"Hey, dude, gotta light?"

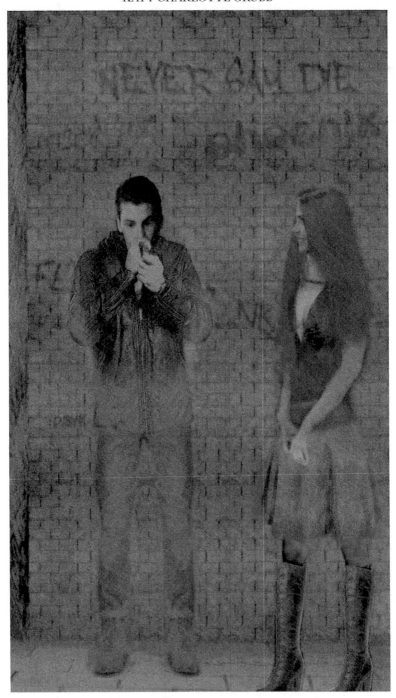

Will turned around to offer his lighter, and then he recognised the face of the slender brunette standing beside him.

"Oh, hey! I didn't know you guys were here… Is—" But before Will could finish, he was sucker-punched from behind.

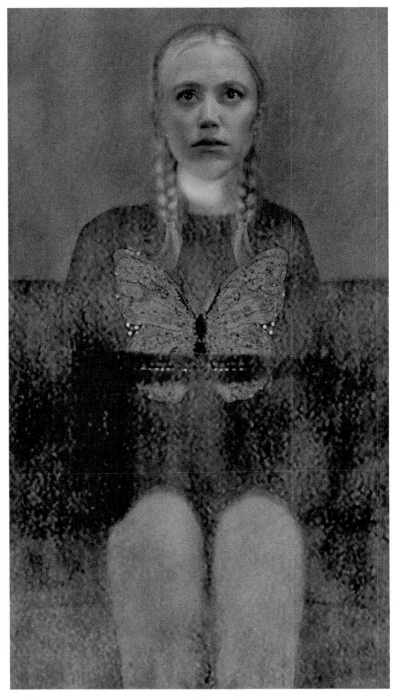

3.

Carla was the first to come round. Her initial impulse was to move her arms, but they were bound tightly behind her; for some time, it seemed, as her wrists and forearms had gone dead.

With difficulty, Carla managed to manoeuvre herself until she was sitting upright on the leatherette couch. As her eyes adjusted to the dark, she gazed around the room trying to make sense of the situation.

On the couch opposite, she could see two guys were propped up. They had been leant against each other as though posed for a picture. Their faces were shrouded by trucker caps, and the LED logos on their t-shirts gave them an eerie spectral glow. Neither stirred.

Then, a few feet away, Carla noticed another figure, a girl laying slumped against the armrest. She was wearing denim overalls over a t-shirt, her long dark hair tied back in a high ponytail. A home-made friendship bracelet hung loosely around her left wrist. It was Ashley.

Seeing her friend in these unfamiliar clothes,

drew Carla's attention to her own strange attire: a long-sleeved navy-blue top with a butterfly depicted in sequins across the front and low-rise rhinestone bedazzled blue jeans. Her hair had been braided into pigtails, secured with leopard print hair-ties.

Carla cringed inwardly at the childish clothes and accessories, and then a terrible realisation dawned. Whoever had brought them here had... (*untied her halter top and was now peeling off her bikini bottoms*). Carla began to tremble violently (*coolness on her bare flesh*). Waves of anger and revulsion welling up (*just throw everything in the trash bag*), her chest constricting tighter (*won't be needing those anymore*) and tighter (*hand me that shirt and the rhinestone jeans*) until she was struggling to breathe.

In the midst of her panic, Carla remembered a breathing technique she'd learned back when she used to do yoga in high school. *Kumbhaka Pranayama, that was it. Breath retention.* Carla inhaled deeply and held it for three seconds before letting it out. She then repeated the pattern, each time holding her breath a few seconds longer before exhaling. Gradually her

breathing resumed its steady automated rhythm.

Just then, Ashley shifted slightly, murmuring something in her sleep. As Carla turned to look at her friend, she found her mind drifting back to the day they met.

It was the first day of school, twelve years ago. She had been seven, and Ashley six. Ashley had recently moved to the States with her parents and her little brother Bruce from London, due to her dad's work transfer.

Despite Ashley's mother being American, Ashley and Bruce both spoke with strong British accents, and at recess, the other kids teased her by making out they couldn't understand a word she said. Carla, strong-willed even as a little girl (in the Barrie family, particularly being the middle child, the only way to make yourself heard was to be louder and more forceful than anyone else), had charged right into the middle of the group and told them to knock it off. She'd taken Ashley under her wing then, and from that day on they had been inseparable.

Now, watching Ashley's slumbering form, thinking of the matching friendship bracelet on her own wrist, Carla forced herself to regain composure. She had to be strong for both herself and Ashley, she didn't intend to let these people, whoever they were, hurt them more than they already had.

4.

"Now put your hands together for Lolly, Roxie, Marky-Mark, Ricky and Polka-Dot Pete... The Gigglers!" a voice boomed from the theatre's PA system.

The Gigglers then came out to their theme tune and proceeded to execute their choreographed dance.

"Welcome, welcome to The Gigglers' Reunion show!" said Marky-Mark, grinning broadly.

"And," added Ricky, "do we have a fun-packed show for you today! But, before we get started — first let's meet our very special guests: Ashley, Carla, Will and Harry!

Numb with shock, Ashley's eyes squinted against the glare of the lights as they were shunted onto the stage by Polka-Dot Pete. Beyond the illuminated set, all she could see was a black abyss.

Nothing about this situation felt real, ever since she had woken up in that room with Carla and the two guys. Woken up? Perhaps this was all a horribly vivid

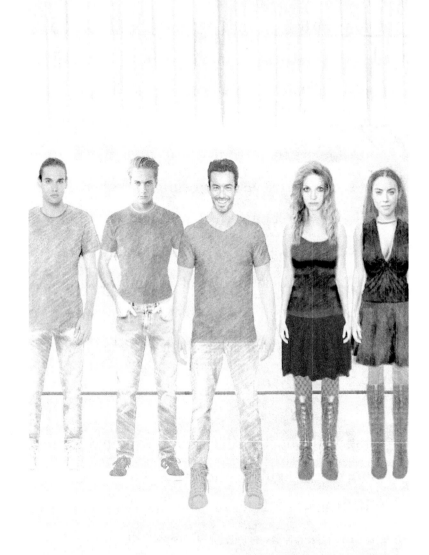

nightmare brought on by that PopRush article that she'd been reading. Could this all be a dream? She felt Carla's hand in hers and gave it a squeeze. It felt solid and firm.

"Now," said Marky, walking to the front of the stage, "are you ready to *jump*?"

"Yeah!" a pre-recorded 'audience' roared from the speakers.

"Are you ready to *jive*?"

"*Yeah!*"

"I can't *hear* you!" called Marky with mock impatience.

"*Yeeeeaaaah!!!*"

"Mark," said Ricky, cupping his hands behind his ears. "Did you hear something?"

"Yeah," replied Marky. "A *pin* drop." There were howls of laughter at this Abbott and Costello routine.

"Me neither! I think I'm going *deaf*!"

Polka-Dot Pete entered the stage, holding a bullhorn. He stopped right beside Ricky's ear and blew. Ricky

doubled over.

"All right," said Marky. "I guess *that's* not it!" He paused. "Now, let's try this again… *are you ready to jive?*"

The 'audience' boomed with volume and elation.

"Well," said Marky. "Let's get this party started!"

The Gigglers assumed the formation and Marky pointed to the ceiling, indicating for an unseen DJ to play the song. The track started, and Marky began to rap: "Step to the left. Twist to the right. Shimmy all around. Ya got it? All right!"

"Hey, hey, hey," Pete interrupted. "Hold the phone!"

"What's up, Pete?"

"Our new friends aren't joining in!"

Marky turned to Roxie, Lolly and Ricky. "Well, we can't have that… can we, guys?"

"Maybe they're feeling shy," said Ricky.

"Is that it?" Marky asked. "Are you guys feeling shy? Come on, you know *Jump N' Jive!*" He walked over to Ashley and Carla. "You sent in such a sweet letter asking to be on the show… Hey, how'd it go again?"

An envelope fell from a large metal chute hanging

from the ceiling, Lolly and Roxie opened it, took out the letter, and started to read it aloud in over-the-top fan girlie squeals — "Hi, Gigglers! My name is Ashley and I'm ten and a half years old," Lolly gushed. "I live in Danbury with my mum, my dad, my little brother Brucie and my turtles Roxie and Pete. We used to have a puppy too. Me and my best friend Carla are your biggest fans ever!"

Ashley felt her stomach clench. The words: *Mum. Dad. Brucie.* The people she loved most in the world.

"We watch The Gigglers *every* day after school," drawled Roxie. "It is the awesomest, amazingest, coolest, funnest show ever! We want to be on The Gigglers sooooooo bad. We know all the songs by heart. Please please please write back. Lots and lots of love from Ashley and Carla."

They both fell about giggling.

"Now then," said Marky, looking directly at Carla. "If you 'know all the songs by heart' then why aren't you joining in, huh?"

"What the fuck is this?" Carla protested. "You guys

are fucking cra—"

Polka-Dot Pete smacked her in the mouth with a mallet prop. "Watch your mouth. This is a family show."

The mallet was cushioned with padding so it didn't cause as much damage as a regular one, but the force of the blow was enough to send Carla staggering backwards into Ashley, and when she ran her tongue over her rapidly-swelling bottom lip she could taste a trickle of blood.

She didn't cry.

Marky continued, eyeing each of the captives in turn.

"*Now… Are. You. Ready. To. Jump. And. Jive?*"

5.

"All right! Now that everybody's in the party mood! You're gonna twist your body, like a corkscrew! Lean to the right, jump up, and back! Strut three times, and clap clap clap!"

Eight-year-old Piper sat in the second row, barely able to contain her excitement. 'Jump N' Jive' was her all-time favourite Gigglers' song ever, and she couldn't believe that she was sitting just a few feet away from *Marky-Mark*!

When she'd entered the competition in Tiger Beat, she'd never expected *her* drawing of The Gigglers to be chosen. But then when the letter came in the mail, and that nice lady from TVNow had called to ask which Saturday she would like to come see the show, and then this morning when the limo arrived to take her to the TV studio where The Gigglers lived in their Giggler Clubhouse…

Piper wished her parents had been able to come, but the lady who was looking after her — Jenna, was very nice. During the break, Jenna said that she would

take her to meet Marky-Mark so Piper could get her Gigglers CD signed. Also, she could give him the special fan letters she'd written. There was one for Marky, and one for Ricky; who was Piper's second favourite Giggler.

She held the CD and the two glitter-covered envelopes tightly in her lap (taking care not to bend them), as the next skit, 'Cooking with Lolly & Roxie' began. They were meant to be making a cake for the rest of The Gigglers, but they weren't doing a very good job.

Piper giggled when Lolly dropped the carton of eggs, and she giggled even more when a whole sack of flour was poured down the chute onto Roxie. Then, when Marky-Mark, Ricky and Polka-Dot Pete ran onto the stage and started sliding around in the flour and eggs, Piper laughed so hard her tummy ached.

⋈

In the wings, Pete was getting ready to explode. In fact, he had been on edge all day. He and Ricky had got heavily drunk the night before and they didn't get

to sleep till it was gone five. Then they had to be on the set for nine-thirty. Pete decided to go along to Marky's dressing room during the break. There was no way he was going to get through this long-ass day without a little pick-me-up.

Now he was trying to wipe off some of the eggy-floury mess, but all he was managing to do was smear it around. "Jesus fucking Christ. I'm covered in this fucking stuff!"

"Cut," Cary yelled from his perch. "And Pete, your mic's still on. Watch your mouth, dammit. This is a family show!"

Flipping Cary the bird, Pete made his way offset to go and get changed.

Jenna stood with her hand on Piper's shoulder in the middle of the bustling corridor. "Let's wait here a while, sweetie. See if we can spot Marky-Mark anywhere."

She then looked down at Piper, who had gone very quiet. "What's the matter, honey? Feelin' nervous?"

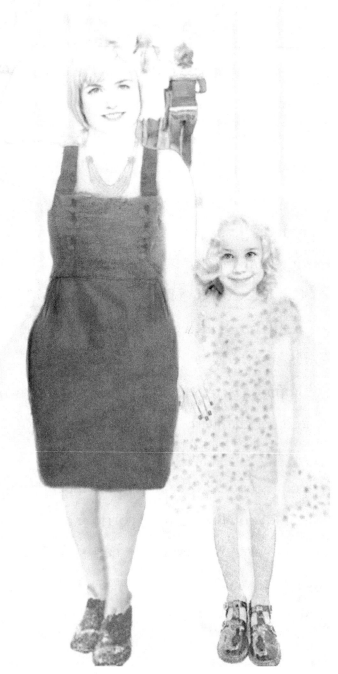

Piper nodded, and Jenna gave her shoulder a squeeze. "Don't be. Marky-Mark is very nice. You'll see."

☙

Marky and Ricky were walking towards Marky's dressing room when they heard Jenna's southern screech rising above the din — "Hey, you two! Got a minute?"

Exchanging a quick side-eye, they strolled over to where Jenna was standing with a little girl by her side.

"Anything for you, Jenna!" Marky tipped her a wink, smiling at Piper.

Jenna blushed, and then quickly recovered. "This is Piper. And she is just a super fan of The Gigglers!" She turned to Piper. "Isn't that right? Especially of yours, Mark."

Piper looked down at her Mary-Janes.

'*Very shy*', Jenna mouthed. Unnecessarily.

Marky nodded, and bent down to meet Piper's eye-level. "Hi, Piper!"

Piper looked up and gave him a smile.

"Did you enjoy the show?" asked Ricky.

She nodded.

"Oh, fab. What was your favourite number?"

Marky gave him a stern look. *Come on, man.* He was holding in a giggle. "I'll bet I can guess?"

Piper looked up at Marky, her eyes shining.

"Jump N' Jive?"

Piper's jaw dropped open slightly as she nodded vigorously. Marky winked at her.

Jenna was getting impatient now. "And Piper was wondering if you could please sign her Greatest Hits CD?"

"Sure thing!"

Marky took out the CD cover and signed it, as did Ricky. He then slipped the cover back in the case and returned the CD to Piper.

"Thank you so much," she whispered, quite overwhelmed.

"Anytime."

"And you had something else for Marky-Mark and Ricky, didn't you?" Jenna prompted. She gave Piper a gentle nudge, and Piper handed Marky and Ricky

the envelopes.

"*Woooooow!!*" exclaimed Ricky. "What's this?!"

Piper had fallen silent again… so Jenna volunteered: "Piper wrote both of y'all a gorgeous little ol' letter about how much she loves The Gigglers. Isn't that precious!"

"Aww…" Marky bent down to kiss Piper on the cheek. "Thank you, honey."

ᐳᐊ

Jenna leant down and scuttled Piper along, holding her hand up and physically making her wave 'bye-bye'.

Ricky waved back to Piper, who was blushing furiously now. "Bye, little nugget! Send my love to your sister-wives!"

Once they had turned the corner, Marky elbowed him, and they shared an impish grin.

Marky shook his head. "You're going straight to hell."

"Isn't that *precious*," mimicked Ricky. He held out his hand to Marky like an airline steward. "Recycling? Composting? Paper waste…?"

Marky pretended to think for a moment before handing over his letter. "Hmmm, just this. Make sure that *doesn't* go in the recycling."

"Oh, my stars," Ricky gasped. "You monster!"

Marky shrugged. "What am I supposed to be here, Santa Claus?"

Ricky unceremoniously chucked the envelopes in the trash and gave him a coquettish smile. "If I get to be the Mrs.?"

"I swear we're not paid enough to deal with this shit," said Marky, before spitting into the trash can.

"Not even close," Ricky agreed. Then he paused, looking around them to make sure they were out of hearing range. "Hey, Santa, did you get those toys?"

"In my dressing room, sugar."

They traded an excited, impatient glance before breaking into a speed-walk down the corridor. As they were turning around the corner towards Marky's dressing room, Lolly stopped them — grabbing Marky by the arm.

"Have you guys seen Roxanne?"

She sounded concerned.

Ricky rolled his eyes.

"We were all in the same fucking place thirty seconds ago, L," Marky said huffily. Break was rapidly ticking away and he had better things to do than get involved in the latest episode of 'The Lauren & Roxanne Show'.

"Yes," Lolly retorted. "I know that. But did you *see* where she went?"

"Sorry," he said, shrugging.

"Well, if you do, can you please tell her I'm—"

"*Fine!*"

Lolly shot them a glare, but they were already gone, slinking off into Marky's dressing room. Lolly stopped in the middle of the corridor, feeling frustrated and anxious.

Pete passed her with a determined gait. Gavin was in hot pursuit, clutching a walkie-talkie and yelling after him to stop. Pete then broke into a jog, and he gave up.

"That kid really wants to try me?" Gavin muttered. "Good luck with that. Good fucking luck." He shook his head and turned around, back towards the set

when… "*Hey!*"

Roxie had just knocked straight into him.

"Oh my god, my bad!" She turned to squeeze his arm without really stopping and ran off giggling down the hallway.

She continued on and saw Lolly, mouthing '*oh my god*' and putting her finger to her lips in a shushing gesture.

"*What?*" Lolly whispered. "Where are you going?"

Roxie kissed her on the cheek and carried on her way to Marky's dressing room. She slouched in front of it and knocked as though in Morse code: *short, short, long*. She looked at Lolly as she waited, still smiling, but oddly, not seeing. Momentarily, the door cracked open, just wide enough for her to squeeze in.

Lolly's eyes narrowed, seething now. *She walked to the door, paused for a moment, and then copied the same knock. When the door opened, she slipped inside.*

6.

Carla, Will, Ashley and Harry sat huddled together on the couches in the Greenroom where they'd been dumped while The Gigglers took their five-minute break.

At first, they sat in silence (ignoring the colourful array of tween magazines, bowls of jelly beans, gummi bears and other candies spread out on the coffee table), hardly daring to move.

It was only after the Gigglers' voices trailed out of earshot, and they felt safe, that they began to talk.

☒

"What the fuck is going on here?" Carla erupted. "I was at the pool. *The pool!* Looking at the water… so peaceful… And then…"

Ashley and Harry were listening intently, waiting for her to finish the story.

"And *then?*" prodded Ashley.

"*And then,* I was jumped from behind and *my own towel* was *pinned* over my face… it smelled like… I don't know… chloroform or some shit… *Then, I remember they…*"

Carla became aware of the damp SoftFlex flooring beneath her. The sharp whiff of disinfectant. The pool locker room. She was being dragged… by her arms through the locker room. Carla tried to force her eyes open, but the fluorescent lighting was searingly bright. Behind her, she could hear the indistinct voices of the men pulling her along the floor…

"Could you make out a face?" Harry asked. "Register height, weight? Hair colour? Who was it exactly?"

"It was aliens," Will muttered under his breath.

"I dunno," said Carla, exasperated. "I-I think I passed out again and then I wake up in this… this fucking *costume*. And where the fuck are—"

"Shut up, dammit," hissed Will. "Just shut up. Do you want them to come back in here?"

Carla shut up.

"Look," Will continued, "sorry, I hate to be the bearer of bad news, but I think it's fairly obvious that these people are totally batshit and the last thing we wanna do is set them off. This is a hostage situation. We're hostages."

"That's pretty sound advice," Harry agreed.

Ashley was shaking her head. "I just can't get over the fact that we've been *kidnapped* by *The Gigglers*... I mean, Roxie and Lolly..."

She paused for a moment. Pensive.

"Ash," interjected Carla.

"But *Marky-Mark*? I had the biggest crush on him! Remember, Carla, that life-size poster I had on my wall? Oh god, this is insane, they're psychopaths." Ashley's eyes widened with horror. "Roxie and Pete? I named my turtles after psychopaths!"

"Jesus, *Ash*," Carla said, giving Ashley a shake. "Focus much? God, that letter..."

"Me too," said Will.

Carla stared at him. "You too, what?"

"I wrote in to be on the show... when I was fourteen. Not to be a guest, didn't have time for that. To be one of The Gigglers." Will started rapping: "Step to the left. Twist to the right. Shimmy all around——"

"Oh my *god*... just stop!" Carla snapped. She winced in pain. "God, my mouth. Is it still bleeding? What are they going to do to us? How the fuck are we going to

get out of this? Are they going to…?"

Her unfinished question hung in the air.

Ashley was starting to cry now, and Carla reached out an arm to try and comfort her.

They all sat in silence for a few moments.

Then, Harry spoke. "You have to play the game. That's the only way any of us are going to get out of this. We have to play *their* game."

Will looked at him, half accusing, half curious. "So, what's your story, huh? You've been pretty quiet so far. Did you write in to be on the show too?"

They could now hear a clamour of voices coming down the corridor.

"Not exactly…"

Then, before Harry could elaborate…

><

…the door opened, and Ricky, Lolly and Roxie burst in.

"Guys n' gals, guys *n' gals*," Ricky drawled, gesturing like a sideshow entertainer addressing a crowd.

Carla, Will, Ashley and Harry sat frozen now as

they desperately tried to avoid meeting the gaze of their captors.

"More like guys and *dolls*, huh, Rox?" Lolly said, eyeing up Carla and Ashley.

Roxie smiled from one to the other. "How're you guys doing?"

Carla glared at her, while Ashley looked fixedly down into her lap. Roxie pulled a face at Carla, then, chuckling to herself, she turned to give Will a wink, but he refused to meet her eye. Her attention stayed on him only momentarily before she was off, surveying the room with the eye of a predator.

Ricky strolled over to where Harry was sitting woodenly in the corner of the couch. His face was blank. Ricky patted him on the shoulder. "How's it going, Harry?"

"Um, fine." Harry nodded slightly, and then turned away.

><

Giving Carla a long hard stare, Lolly moved over to Ashley. She perched on her lap, and then leaning

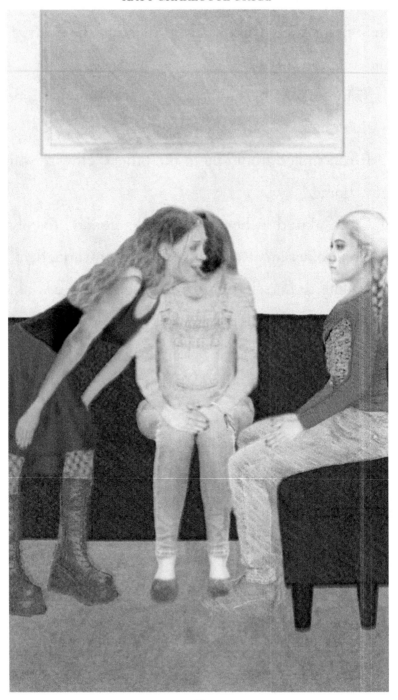

in close (so close Lolly imagined she could hear the younger girl's heartbeat), she began to stroke Ashley's cheek.

Bristling at Lolly's touch, Ashley started fretfully smoothing out the tassel on her pink and white lanyard friendship bracelet, the little plastic beads clinking together between her fingers.

"*Carla*," Ashley whispered. Her voice came out as a strangled rasp.

Their eyes met and Carla shook her head.

Say nothing.

It was then that Lolly noticed the matching bracelets. "Cute," she said, turning to Carla. "Did you make these at a sleepover?"

Before Carla could respond, Marky and Pete entered the room.

"Howdy," said Marky. "You guys have a nice break?"

"Screw you," Carla said, jumping to her feet.

Pete grabbed her by the shoulders. "I'm not gonna tell you again."

"Well," said Marky, "we'd better get back to the

stage. We don't wanna keep our audience waiting."

A kind of numbness had settled over Harry while they were in the Greenroom. Now, as he and the others were being marched away towards the stage, Harry felt as though he were falling in slow motion, tumbling ever deeper into this waking nightmare.

Then he felt a hand on his arm.

"Harry?"

It was Ashley.

"Yeah?"

"What are they going to do to us?"

Harry shook his head. "I don't know, Ashley."

"Will they let us go?"

"I don't *know*, Ashley."

"Hey," said Pete. "You two shut up and keep walking. No whispering. I mean it. I don't want to hear you talk."

Heads bowed, Ashley and Harry continued walking in silence. *It was only when Harry glanced up briefly that he noticed Marky was watching him with an odd half-smile on*

his face.

7.

"Dad! Hey, Dad, wait up!"

Glenn Ferrier turned around to see his twelve-year-old son Harry running down the hallway towards him.

Glenn shook his head in exasperation. "Jesus, Harry. Not now, okay?" He then carried on his way without giving Harry so much as a backwards glance.

Harry sighed.

Once again, he'd been given the brush off.

As Harry walked despondently, scuffing his sneakers on the rubber floor, he found himself thinking angrier and angrier thoughts about his dad.

He was just a *jerk*, that was all. A great big mean old super-jerk, who didn't care about him one tiny bit. The only times his dad paid Harry any attention were when he was nagging him about his homework (which he had to complete in a dressing room at TVNow every day after school), his grades, and eating enough vegetables. The rest of the time it was just work, work, work. Nonstop.

Harry kicked at the skirting board running along the

corridor, chipping the paint. *Good. Stupid Dad… stupid TVNow… stupid* everything.

Then Harry paused — outside the door of Marky-Mark's dressing room.

Harry liked Marky; in fact, he liked *all* the Gigglers. Unlike his dad, they always had time for him, and they played all sorts of games together when they weren't filming. Though the past weeks even they had been oddly distant with him. Not exactly unfriendly, but distant all the same.

Nevertheless, he knocked on the door and without waiting for an answer, he opened it and went inside.

><

Harry peeped around the corner of the l-shaped room, open-mouthed at the scene before him.

Ricky was swigging from a bottle of some kind of liquor, while Marky was leaning over the dressing table; he held a plastic straw to one nostril, and he was *sniffing* a line of white powder up the straw into his nose.

But what stunned Harry the most was seeing *Lolly* sitting half-naked, leant against Roxie, wearing only

her jeans and a bra.

Just then, Marky looked up and saw him. "Hey, bud." Marky smiled. "How's it goin'?"

"Oh, sorry," said Harry, taken aback.

Flattered though he was at Marky's welcome, Harry felt a strange uneasy feeling in the pit of his stomach without quite knowing why.

"Sorry," he repeated, flashing a nervous smile at the other Gigglers; all of whom were looking at him now. "I'm just gonna go."

Harry turned to leave, but before he could do so, Pete entered the room; shutting the door behind him.

He was trapped.

"Hey," said Roxie. "Where you goin'? Stay and hang out with us." She gestured for Harry to come closer. Tentatively, he did so, and Roxie pulled him onto her lap, jiggling him like a baby.

"So, kiddo," said Marky amiably. "What've you been up to? It's been a while since we've all rapped."

"Um, yeah," Harry faltered. "Not much, just, you know... stuff!" All he wanted to do right then was get

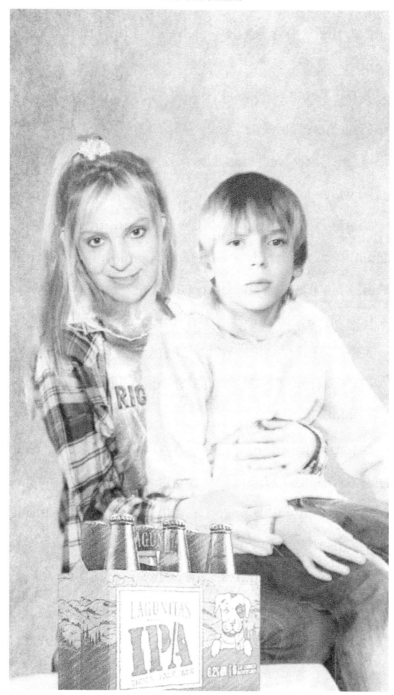

out of there, but Roxie was holding him that bit too tightly.

"Hey, hey, hey," Ricky soothed. "Relax. How old are you now, eleven?"

"Um… twelve," said Harry.

"Twelve… wow!" exclaimed Ricky, looking around at Marky, Lolly, Roxie and Pete. "I had my first drink when I was twelve. It was Veuve Clicquot. Bottoms up, y'all!" He handed the bottle to Pete. "Hey, Pete, why don't you pour little Harry a drink?"

"No," Harry spluttered. "Uh, thanks, but I'm okay."

Harry winced as Pete filled a small glass and pressed it into his hand.

It had a funny smell as he brought the rim of the glass to his lips. Then Harry took a sip, and grimaced. *Ugh*, it was awful! It tasted a little like hairspray and it made his throat burn.

The Gigglers tittered with amusement.

"Whoo-hoo!" Marky applauded. "Big man!"

Still reeling, Harry pointed over at the remains of the white powder on the table. "What is… that?" he

asked timidly.

"Nose candy," cooed Roxie, planting a kiss on the crown of his head.

"Just something to keep our energy up," said Pete. "What with your *daddy* working us so damn hard without a single fucking day off."

Harry flinched at the sudden aggression.

Lolly placed a hand on his shoulder. "Now, your dad wouldn't be very happy if he found out you'd been drinking, would he?"

Harry shook his head. He could well imagine what Dad would say. His dad never hit him, but he shouted when he got really mad, and usually ended up making Harry cry.

He felt like crying now.

"So," Lolly continued. "No telling Dad any crazy stories, right?"

Harry nodded.

"Our secret?" pressed Roxie, her arms tightening around him.

"Yes," he pleaded, fighting back tears. "Our secret.

I won't tell anyone, I swear."

Roxie released her grip.

"Okay, buddy," said Marky. "You'd better run along before everybody starts wondering where you are."

Harry didn't need telling twice. He leapt off Roxie's lap and raced towards the door.

"Bye, Harry," said Lolly.

"A toute a l'heure, enfant," Ricky called.

Roxie smiled, giving him a wave.

Pete opened the door and stepped aside, then, before Harry could run out, Pete touched his arm. "Now remember our secret. We don't want you getting in trouble with your dad."

⋈

Harry ducked out of the room into the corridor. He stood and leant against the wall for a moment, shaking, before he turned and ran off.

8.

"Now it's tiiime for The Race Against Sliiime!" Marky *announced, as two pieces of set rolled apart on the stage to reveal an obstacle course.* The course included tunnels to crawl through and a gunge-filled inflatable pool with two balancing beams across it. "And our first contestants are Ashley and Will!"

Ricky and Pete jostled Ashley and Will forward; they were both terrified and disorientated as they had been tightly blindfolded.

"It's not going to be easy, you guys," Marky continued, "as you can see, they can't see a thing." He gestured to Pete and Ricky who began to push Will and Ashley, twirling them around, and ignoring their cries of protest. "They will have to rely on their teammates to guide them through the course. Whoever completes The Race Against Slime first, wins! And tell us, Lolly, what are the amaaaaazing prizes we're giving away?"

"Well, Marky…" Lolly beamed. "Today, not only will our lucky winners be taking home a box of Silly Sand, but they will be the envy of all their friends

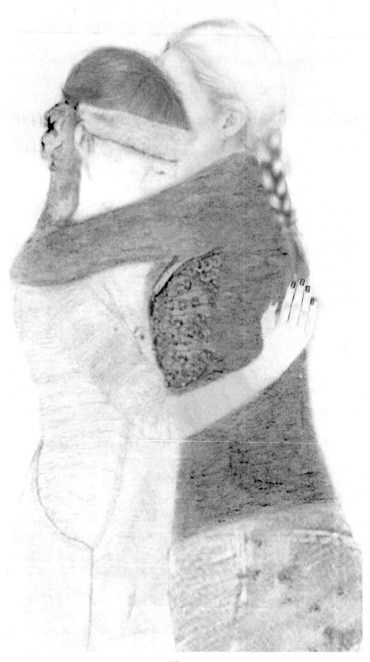

with the official Gigglers' back-to-school stationery set and… wait for it… thanks to our awesome sponsor — Toys 'R' Us, we're also giving away a $100 Toys 'R' Us Gift Card!"

There was a loud explosion of cheering and whooping from the 'audience'.

✄

Ashley was sobbing as Carla tried her best to console her.

"Ashley," said Carla, drawing her in for a hug. "Ashley, baby. You need to be stronger than this, okay?"

"But they—" Ashley started before collapsing into fresh floods of tears behind her blindfold.

"Don't even think about them," interrupted Carla. "Just don't think about them. Now you need to stop crying and listen to me. Okay?"

Ashley took a shuddery breath and nodded.

"All right. Now, at the start of the course is a tunnel you crawl through, and you follow it around. Then, at the end of the tunnel is a ramp with a rope that you climb up. At the top of the ramp is a balancing beam

over a pool; you walk across that and you're finished, okay?" Carla gave Ashley another squeeze. "I love you so much. You are my sister and my best friend, and I *know* you can do this."

Ashley gave Carla a kiss on the cheek before she was wrenched away by Pete and taken to the start of the course.

The klaxon sounded and Ashley set off crawling, feeling her way through the canvas tunnel. She tried to tune out the hyena-like cackles of The Gigglers and just focus on the sound of Carla's voice calling out instructions.

Reaching the end of the tunnel, she felt around for the length of knotted rope; and grabbing it, she began to hoist herself up the ramp.

"Come on, Ashley," shouted Carla. "You are doing so well!"

ﭏ

Ashley was now gingerly crossing the beam, toes pointed and arms outstretched.

"Come on," Carla urged again. "You can do this,

64

baby. You're almost there."

She was.

Carla watched as Ashley took another cautious step, just a couple more and she would make it — then suddenly, Roxie reached out and shoved Ashley off the beam into the gunge.

Alarmed by Ashley's scream, Will lost his balance and fell into the pool too. They stumbled about, slipping and sliding around in the gunge, as Roxie and Lolly collapsed into howls of raucous laughter.

Carla lunged forward to go to Ashley's aid, but she was restrained by Pete and Ricky. All Carla could do was stand back helpless, as she watched her friend growing more and more distressed to the accompaniment of taunts and jeering from Lolly and Roxie.

Ashley was sitting up to her waist in lukewarm slime trying desperately to remove her blindfold, however, it was triple knotted so tightly that it just wouldn't budge.

Ashley tried to stand up. She spread her arms out, reaching for something to hold on to, but there was nothing and Ashley's feet kept sliding out from under

her, slipping on the rubber floor.

"Aww…" Roxie crouched down next to the pool and called over to Ashley, "Here, honey. Let me help you up."

Ashley turned in the direction of Roxie's voice.

"Here," said Roxie, straightening up and extending her arm. "Take my hand…"

Warily, Ashley struggled again to get to her feet, groping through the air until she found Roxie's hand. She was just about to grab it when Roxie yanked her hand away and Ashley fell backwards, landing hard on her butt.

This was the final straw for Carla. "Leave her alone, you fucking bitch!"

Roxie and Lolly froze.

"Whoa, whoa, whoa, *really*?" Roxie stared at her, instantly breaking character. "Really? You asked for a bitch? Did you just ask for a bitch?!"

Ricky and Pete let go of Carla as Lolly strode over and grabbed her by the arm; then, twisting it behind her back, Lolly dragged Carla up to Roxie. Roxie spat

in Carla's face.

"Not smart," said Lolly. "*At all.*"

Carla winced and began to hyperventilate as Lolly held her still for Roxie, who wound her right arm back to deliver a slap.

"The Bitch is here now," said Roxie. "The bitch is *here.*"

Roxie started slapping Carla in a frenzy, completely out of control, while Lolly gave her quick kicks to the groin. After an excruciating minute, they ran out of steam and stepped back from Carla's curled, crying, and aspirating figure on the floor.

"I'm getting real tired of her little mouth," said Pete. "Ricky, take her out."

Ricky flashed a big shit-eating stage grin, and then grabbing Carla by the arms, he began to drag her offstage as she screamed and cursed. Harry gestured helplessly in protest, while Will and Ashley floundered around in the gunge pool, blind and terrified.

Ricky ignored them, shoving Harry out the way as he and Carla exited the stage. He hadn't been known

as the jock on the show for nothing.

Marky and Pete guided Ashley and Will out of the pool, jovially removing their blindfolds. It was business as usual for them.

"Carla," Ashley wailed. "Oh god, Carla." She made a move towards the wings, but Marky grabbed her by the shoulder. Tenderly yet meaningfully he put his finger to her lips, warning her to be quiet.

Momentarily the screaming stopped, and Ricky strutted back onstage. He had turned on his Gigglers' persona again. It was an ability they had all perfected over the years; handily, as though flicking a switch.

⚭

Marky now stood flanked by Ashley and Will, with an arm around each of their shoulders. "Now," he said, "as neither of you guys completed The Race Against Slime, sadly you can't win the Silly Sand or the Toys 'R' Us Gift Card. But… you do get the official Gigglers' back-to-school stationery set and an official Gigglers' t-shirt."

Polka-Dot Pete was brandishing his mallet prop.

"Thanks," said Ashley flatly. "That's awesome."

"Cheers," Will murmured.

Lolly then skipped over to present them with their prizes — a t-shirt emblazoned with The Gigglers' logo, and brightly coloured Lisa Frank-style Gigglers' themed stationery.

They thanked her dutifully.

"Now," said Marky, "we're going to take a short break. And then when we come back, it's time for 'Up Close & Personal', where we get to chat with our special guests!"

Ricky and Pete rolled in a huge brightly coloured bondage wheel from offstage, placing it slightly behind the chute. Then Lolly, Roxie, Ricky and Pete hustled Harry, Will and Ashley (carrying the prizes) off the stage, and back to the Greenroom.

9.

Marky was alone in the dressing room where they had stashed their coats and bags. He was singing 'Got the Giggles', posing and dancing in front of the mirror — checking himself out from different angles.

"You know that feelin' when the giggles take hold? You feel it in your head, right down to your toes," Marky sang. "It's utterly outrageous. It's too contagious. It tingles through your body and you lose control."

"What are you doing?" asked Lolly, barely stifling a laugh.

Marky jumped, whirling around to face her. "Jesus Christ, Lauren! Don't fucking sneak up on me like that." He paused. "How long have you been standing there?"

"I just walked in," said Lolly, quickly composing herself. "Sorry." She looked at him, genuinely curious. "So, what were you doing?"

Marky was quiet for a moment. "Can I ask you something?"

"Sure."

"You know… it's been like ten years. A long time. I'm older… that strict fitness regime I had, well kind of fell by the wayside… and—"

Lolly stopped him. "Mark, you look great. You seriously have nothing to worry about. Okay?"

"Thanks, L."

"Now snap out of it. Put your game face on—"

Just then, Roxie, Pete and Ricky came in.

"So, they're both changing now," Ricky said. "Supposed to clean up too, but I'll be the judge on whether that worked out for them."

"Nice fake-out with the little one, Rox," said Pete. "That was boss."

"Believe me." Roxie smirked. "She had it coming." She looked to Lolly. "Right, L?"

"*Damn right,*" said Lolly. "She's gonna learn the hard way not to screw with us."

"So, Mark," Ricky said, tapping his watch. "Yeah, I told them ten minutes."

Marky nodded. "Yeah. You and Pete go and get Will. L, Rox and I will be waiting onstage."

"Ten-four," said Pete.

Will had wiped off most of the gunk from his face and hands. Now he was frantically pulling on the shirt and jeans that Ricky had given him.

Ashley, on the other hand, was refusing to get changed. "Oh god, Carla. Where is she? What did they..."

Will picked up the clean blouse and jeans given for Ashley to wear and awkwardly tried to reason with her. He wasn't used to seeing girls cry in front of him without feeling in some way responsible. "Yo, yo, yo, uh, Ashley, listen, look I'm sure she's fine, but—"

"*Fine?*" Ashley squawked. "Are you crazy? God, we have to get out of here. We need to *find* her! You don't understand, she's my best friend and she could be lying somewhere hurt or..."

There was a silence, and then, taking a deep breath, Harry tried. "Ashley. I implore you. You have my oath; we will find Carla. We *will* get out of here. But from where I stand, at this moment, the only rational course

of action is to go into that bathroom and change the damn clothes."

Ashley nodded, then taking the blouse and jeans, she scurried into the bathroom. As they heard the water running, Harry and Will glanced at each other in relief.

Moments later, the door opened, and Ricky and Pete strolled in. Ricky gave the room a sweeping glance. "Where's Ashley?"

"Bathroom... changing," said Will.

Pete looked at Harry, who averted his eyes but nodded in agreement. Pete marched across to the bathroom to fetch Ashley, just as she opened the door and stepped back into the room. Her face was washed but she was still wearing the same gunge-covered clothes from before.

"What's this?" said Ricky, looking her up and down. "I thought I told you *both* to be cleaned up and changed before we came back."

Pete grabbed Will by the shoulders and took him out of the room.

"Where's Carla?" Ashley demanded. "What have

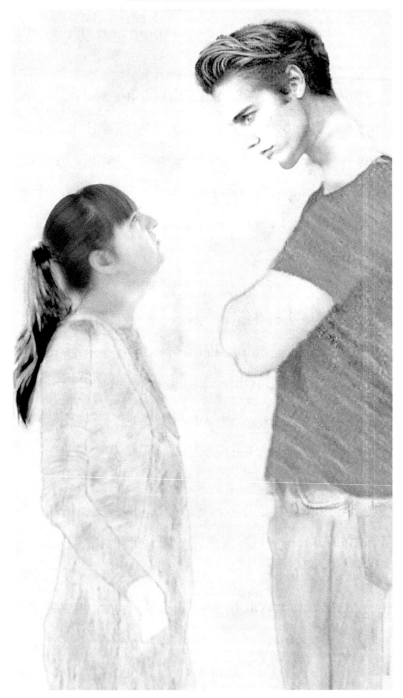

you done with Car—"

"Shhhhh! What did I tell you? Fool me once, shame on you. Fool me twice?" He pointed to the blouse and jeans Ashley was holding. "I expect to see you dressed and ready, with bells on, when we're back." He smiled. "I helped the girls pick that blouse out; they thought it was cute. And that colour is *everything* on you."

Ricky held her gaze for a strange, inscrutable moment and then shrugged.

Ashley rushed back to the bathroom to change.

Ricky winked at Harry before turning to leave.

10.

"Now," Marky said. "It's time for your faaaavourite part of the show… drrrrum roll, please! And our first guest is Will!"

Ricky and Pete brought Will onto the stage. Pinioning his arms to his sides, they bustled him over to the padded bondage wheel where Marky, Lolly and Roxie were waiting.

Forcing Will to climb backwards up onto the metal footrests, Roxie and Lolly proceeded to strap him in. *After securing him tightly, they gave the wheel a spin.*

'Oh, fuck,' *thought Will.*

⋈

Will was sitting at the hotel bar he worked at. He'd finished his shift and was just enjoying a drink with a couple of the guys before setting off home. Craning his head around, he noticed two very familiar faces at one of the nearby tables. Doing a quick double-take, he realised who they were. Surely that was Lolly and Roxie from that old kids' show 'The Gigglers'. With the alcohol in his system lowering his inhibitions, he climbed down from

the barstool and approached them.

They both looked up when they saw Will standing next to their table.

"Well, hey there, cutie," said Roxie.

Will was rather less than starstruck, emboldened by liquid courage. "Hello, ladies…"

"I wouldn't go that far," said Roxie as she reached out her hand to him. Will took her hand and kissed it, bowing slightly to Lolly.

"So," Will said, "I'm gonna feel like a dork if I'm wrong… but you guys *both* look exactly like these actresses."

"Do go on," said Roxie, leaning in towards him.

"The Gigglers. Roxie. And Lolly."

"The *what*? Who?" Lolly raised an eyebrow.

"Really," Roxie said. "Is that meant to be a compliment?"

"Oh. Man. Yes, yes, big time."

"We'll take it then," said Roxie, smiling flirtatiously.

Lolly looked at him blankly. "I still have no idea what he's talking about."

Will turned scarlet.

"Don't pay her any mind," Roxie said. "She's just teasing. So, were you a fan of the show?"

"Yeah, I was *addicted* to it when I was a kid!"

"That's sweet of you," said Lolly. She gestured to the empty chair. "Join us for a round?"

"Sure," Will said.

He sat down, and Lolly poured from a very expensive bottle of wine into two empty glasses, before filling her own with cranberry juice. Will's eyes goggled a bit at the sight of it.

Lolly noticed his reaction. "Fancy, huh? We just charge it to the room."

"This," said Will, "might be one of the best nights of my life."

"Just you wait," Roxie said.

"Stick with us, kid," added Lolly. "So, seeing as you already know who we are… what about you? Do you have a name?"

Will was a little thrown by this, but he quickly recovered. "Um, yeah, I'm Will. Enchanté…"

Lolly giggled.

"Oh, wow," said Roxie. "You *are* a dork. Cute though. So, what brings you to this dump?"

"Actually, I work here… at the bar."

Lolly shot Roxie a look. "Fascinating!"

Seeing Will's face fall, Roxie looked back at her to say, '*Come on, be nice!*'. "Don't mind her," Roxie said to Will. "She's on the wagon." Lolly visibly tensed at the mention, but Roxie ignored her and giggled. "And what's your night looking like?"

Will shrugged. "Nothing planned. I was just gonna head home."

"Head home? It's only *twelve-thirty!*"

"Yeah, man," said Lolly. "Live a little."

"Well…" Will mused.

"Wait," said Roxie. "Hold that thought. I'm just gonna go powder my nose." As Roxie got up from the table, she dropped a cocktail napkin in Will's lap. "Whoops!"

"That's all right," said Will, a little flustered.

She turned and winked at Will before heading for

the bathroom, leaving him sitting alone with a slightly predatory Lolly.

"Don't worry," Will said. "I won't say anything about…" *Wrong move.* "I mean I totally respect that you're…" *Even worse.* "I'll just shut up now."

Lolly stared at him like a detective assessing a potential suspect. "Totally 'addicted' to The Gigglers, were you?"

"Poor choice of words," said Will with a sheepish grin.

"You were a fan of the show? A big fan?"

Will shifted uncomfortably in his seat… "When I was a kid, yeah."

"And how about now?"

Will looked away from her piercing gaze and down into his lap, where he was still holding the dropped cocktail napkin. He bent it a little and noticed a firmness. He swallowed briefly. "Now more than ever."

Lolly registered his look; she'd played this game before. She laughed approvingly. "Good answer."

Then, abruptly she got up, sighed, and left without

a word.

As Will watched her walk away from the table, feeling a little bemused, he took another swig of wine and set the cocktail napkin down on the table. Inside was a paper sleeve containing a plastic swipe card: Roxie and Lolly's room key.

><

Roxie was laid out on the queen-size bed, propped up on her elbows and looking down at Lolly, who was sitting cross-legged on the floor at the foot of the bed.

"I'm so proud of you, baby," said Roxie.

"You're sloshed."

"Maybe." Roxie smiled. "But you're still beautiful."

"Thanks."

"You know," Roxie said. "I'm gonna start going to meetings with you... next week... maybe."

They both laughed at this.

"I just get so *bored* sober."

"There are other ways to have fun." Lolly kneeled up and started caressing Roxie's hair. Roxie kissed her, then she leant back on the bed and sighed.

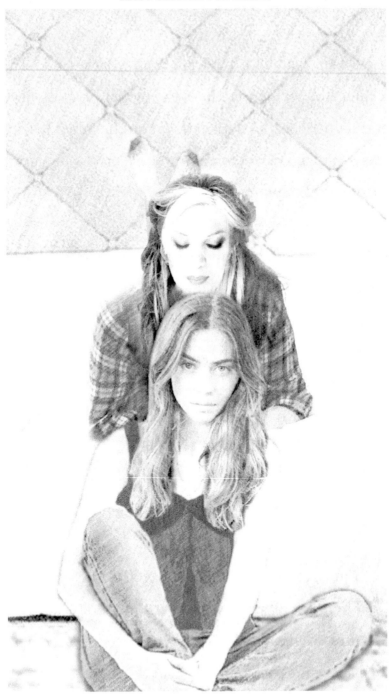

"Yeah. But. I need to be at like a ten. At all times."

"You?" said Lolly. "Never!"

"Hey, you know what would be hot?" Roxie said, sitting up.

Just then they were interrupted by the sound of someone trying to key into their room.

"What the fuck?" said Lolly. "Um, *wrong room…*"

Roxie started giggling, and soon Will had stumbled into the room, now heavily drunk and carrying a bottle of bourbon.

"Why, hullo there," Roxie purred, half excited, half amused at the comedy of errors she had created.

"Hi…" said Will.

Roxie let a shoulder strap slip and began writhing around on the bed, still laughing. Lolly looked on in mild disgust, as Will approached.

"Woah," he said. "You bitches are kinda wild."

Roxie pulled Will in by the shirt collar and started kissing him, causing him to drop the bourbon. She then proceeded to fondle his torso, when Will started to giggle helplessly.

"Ooh," breathed Roxie. "You're ticklish? That's cute…"

Lolly, who had been standing upright, joggling one leg with anxiety, had had enough. She picked up the bottle from beside the bed and took a healthy swig, emptying the bottle and undoing ninety days of sobriety.

"You guys are *selfish*," she said, slurring her words already. "And. You don't know what you're doing."

She jumped in. Roxie kissed her and continued purring. Will was still in slight disbelief at his luck, but he was enjoying every second.

"Where's his phone?" asked Lolly.

"Aw, baby, you're not making any sense," Roxie said, trying to coo her now drunken girlfriend. "Just, come here."

"I wanna know! What's his name again?"

Lolly looked at Will.

"Uh, William, Will…"

"Will," said Lolly. "Isn't this kind of a big deal for you?"

"Yes." Will nodded. "A very. Yes."

"So," said Lolly. *"Get the camera out…"*

11.

The wheel had stopped spinning and Will looked as though he was going to be sick.

"Ladies," said Will. "Ladies… please, can't we talk about this?"

"Oh," said Lolly. "You wanna talk? Hmm… okay, let's talk! What should we talk about… what about the little video you uploaded on RedTube! Yeah, let's talk about that."

"I-I didn't," Will stammered. "I honestly don't have a clue how that video got leaked. Please, you've got to believe—"

"*Buzzzz.*" Lolly imitated a game show buzzer. "Wrong answer!" She nodded to Ricky and Pete, who gave the wheel another spin. "Now, we're going to try this again. What the *fuck* made you think you had the right to *release* a private video of Roxie and me out into the public sphere like that? Why did you do it, huh? *Huh?*"

"Listen," said Will breathlessly. "Please—"

"Were the shaky videos of you jerking off into a sock

failing to get you subscribers?" Roxie asked. "Did you need to use Lolly and I to draw people in?"

"I… uh."

Will fell silent.

"Hmm…" Lolly said. "You know, I don't think Will's feeling very talkative… So, what should we do instead?"

"Hey," said Roxie. "Why don't we all sing a song together!"

"I think that's a *super* idea," Lolly said. "What do you think, guys?"

"How about…" said Marky. "Got the Giggles!!"

At that, a cluster of feathers and other tickling implements fell out of the chute like a piñata.

They each grabbed one. Pete ripped open Will's shirt, Ricky pulled off his sneakers and socks, and The Gigglers started mercilessly tickling him while singing 'Got the Giggles'.

"You know that feelin'?" sang Roxie. "When the giggles take hold?"

"You feel it in your head, right down to your toes,"

Pete sang, as he tickled the soles of Will's feet.

"It's utterly outrageous!"

"It's too contagious!"

"It tingles through your body and you lose control!"

"No," Will panted. "Please! Please stop…"

The Gigglers paused for a moment.

"You know?" said Marky, looking serious. "Maybe we *should* stop."

There was a pause.

Will looked hopeful.

"*Nah!*" sang The Gigglers in unison, and they resumed tickling him.

⋈

Hyperventilating, Will was desperately trying to get his breath back. Lolly stood up close to him, holding a switchblade she had taken out of her pocket.

"You know, Will," Lolly said, "I understand you. *Really*, I do! All this swagger, this whole 'ladies' man' thing you've got going on…" She unbuttoned his jeans and yanked them down, along with his boxers. "It's all just *overcompensating* for your many… *many*

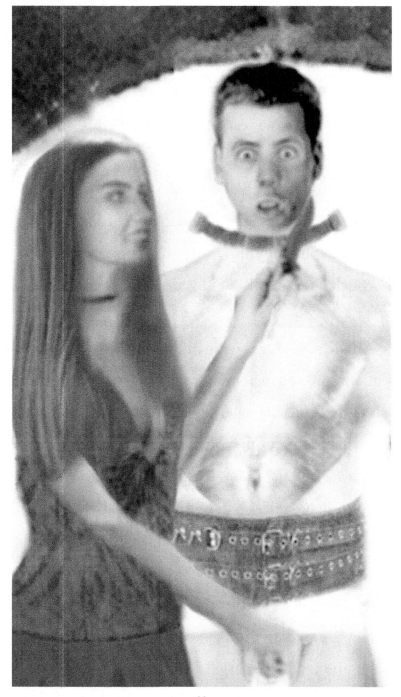

inadequacies."

Grabbing hold of his penis, Lolly clicked open the switchblade and began waving it in the air teasingly.

"*God! No!* Please, you don't have to do this!" begged Will. "I'm sorry, okay… *please!*"

Lolly brought the blade down, slicing off Will's penis in one swoop. She then stuffed the severed appendage into his gaping mouth.

"Suck on that," she said.

><

Ashley and Harry were in the Greenroom. Ashley was now dressed in her new outfit: low-rise jeans, and a navy blue and white checked blouse knotted just above her belly button. 'Jump N' Jive' was playing through the speakers in the room. It finished, and then it started again. The Gigglers had put it on repeat.

"I can't believe," said Ashley through gritted teeth, "that I used to actually *like* that fucking song." She paused for a moment, and then she completely lost it. Ashley jumped up from the couch and ran over to the door. She repeatedly tried turning the doorknob, but

it was locked. Ashley started kicking the door, crying in anger and frustration.

"Those giggling bastards," she bawled. "I swear to *god*, when I get out of here, I am going to take that life-size poster of Marky-fucking-Mark, shred it into confetti, set light to it, and Jump N' Jive on the burning ashes! Let us out of here! *Fuck!*"

Harry ran over and pulled her away from the door. All the rage fell away and she collapsed into his arms. He held her as they went to sit back down on the couch.

"You don't understand the kind of people we're dealing with here," said Harry. "I need to impress that upon you. If you conflate these hoodlums with the characters they played on TV… We're dealing with a criminal element. You all don't *get it*."

"And *you do*, do you?" snapped Ashley. "God, none of this makes any sense. *Why* are they doing this? To us? And where's Carla and Will?"

"Look," Harry said. "I don't know why you, specifically, were targeted…" He hesitated. "But I

know why I was."

"What do you mean?" asked Ashley, softening. "What happened?"

"My dad's Glenn Ferrier."

"Oh…" Ashley processed this; she recognised the name.

"I grew up at the studio. My mom took off when I was three, and good old Glenn never had any time for me. Marky and Ricky, they were like brothers to me, all of them… I remember how we'd sit around playing Uno during their breaks. Lolly, she was like a Mom to me. That's what makes it… what they did… feel like such a betrayal."

Harry paused, choked up with anger and grief at the memory.

"It's okay," said Ashley. "Take your time."

"It's so stupid. Looking back, I can see it. Reading all the stuff online about what was going on. You could *feel* it, you know? The atmosphere onset. But, typical Dad, so focused on churning out episode after episode — if it wasn't on the schedule it wasn't on his radar."

Ashley moved to put an arm around his shoulder, but Harry shook it off. "That day, I remember, I was trying to snatch a few moments of his time when as usual he was… preoccupied. Anyway, I stopped outside Marky's dressing room…"

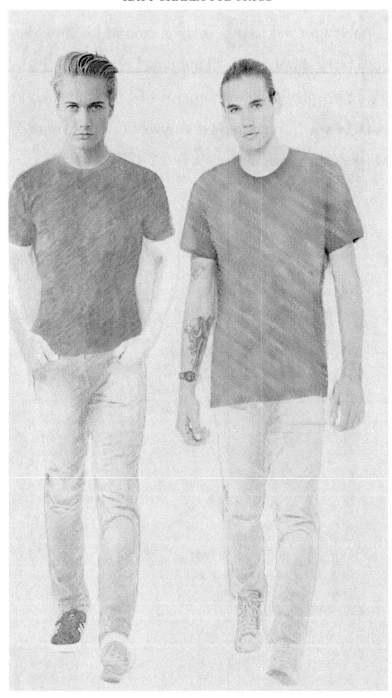

12.

Ricky and Pete were walking down the corridor towards the Greenroom.

"Man," said Ricky. "That was fucking priceless."

"I know," Pete said. "He was crying like a little bitch at the end. *Please, please...* you don't have to do this. I'm sorry, okay! *Oh god*, please... just let me go... waaaaah..."

Ricky sniggered. "What a pussy."

"Damn," said Pete. "This is way more effective than that CBT group therapy crap they forced down my neck when I was on the inside. I swear to god, when I get my hands on that snivelling little rat, Harry, I'm gonna inflict a whole different kinda CBT on him."

Ricky cracked up with laughter. "You know?" he said. "I think this might be the first episode I'm actually enjoying."

"Yeah, me too. Damn... that show was a curse."

"Yeah, tell me about it," said Ricky. "You know there was actually a time when I had aspirations to be a real actor — not just this kiddie entertainment crap?"

"*Aspirations.* That's a pretty big word for you, man."

"Shut up," said Ricky, giving him a playful punch on the shoulder. "But seriously, that's what I'm talkin' about. You know… when I was seventeen during the summer hiatus, I auditioned for a production of 'Twelfth Night'. God, I really wanted to play Sebastian."

"Yeah," Pete said. "I could see that… you'd have rocked it."

"Needless to say, it didn't happen. You know what project I did get cast in that summer? A made-for-TV movie on the Disney channel. My character didn't even have a proper fucking name. He was literally called 'The Jock'. The. Fucking. Jock!"

"Believe me," said Pete. "I get it. You wanna talk about hardship? Try doin' a seven-month stretch with a name like Polka-Dot Pete. Though having said that, they only called me that the once. A couple of swings with the ol' lock-in-a-sock saw to that."

"Yeah, man, what was up with that anyway?"

"Son-of-a-bitch bartender got me kicked out of

Roosters, so I came back later with a bottle of gasoline. It was bullshit, bro; the place was closed up — it's not like anyone got torched."

"Shit," Ricky said. "Sorry, man."

They stopped for a moment next to a door; behind it, they could hear Carla whimpering feebly. Pete barged into the room. There was a heavy thud, a muffled scream, and then silence. Pete walked out looking triumphant.

"Pete, dude," said Ricky, "I gotta hand it to Mark. Putting all this together was fucking genius. How long till we have to be outta here?"

Pete looked at his watch. "Joe, Donny and the others said we need to be gone by seven o'clock… so shit, that only gives us three hours!"

"Better get moving then," Ricky said.

><

In the Greenroom, the music had stopped.

"Those sick fucks," said Ashley. "And you were only twelve? *God*, I'm so sorry."

"Ashley," Harry said. "From here on out we've just

got to comply. I mean it. Don't antagonise them in any way. And then, at the first opportunity, get the hell out of here. Got it?"

"Yeah," said Ashley. She put her arms around Harry. This time, he let her. They were still embracing when Pete and Ricky came into the room.

"Aww…" Pete said, "now isn't that sweet!"

Harry and Ashley sprang apart instantly.

"Come on, Harry," called Ricky cheerfully. "It's your turn now, bud!"

"No, Harry," Ashley cried, getting to her feet.

"Ashley," warned Harry. "It's okay."

Ashley's eyes met his in a moment of silent understanding. She took a deep breath and calmly sat back down.

"Good girl," said Ricky.

Harry walked over to Pete, who was standing by the open door. He allowed Pete to escort him out of the room. Ashley remained silent but her eyes showed her fear.

Ricky moved towards Ashley and she flinched away

from him, but instead, he bent to retrieve a DVD from under the coffee table. It was a compilation of The Gigglers' episodes. "It's okay, honey," he said. "It will all be over soon." Ricky turned to look at her. "Say… that blouse *does* look darling on you!"

Ashley didn't say a word, it was as though she had retreated into herself.

Ricky inserted the disc into the built-in player of the forty-inch flatscreen television mounted on the wall. "Here. This will keep you entertained in the meantime."

Ricky paused, looking at her expectantly.

"Thank you," said Ashley.

He smiled and pressed 'play' on the remote. As he walked over to the door, he turned to give her a little wave. "See you later then!"

He left, locking the door behind him.

⋈

The DVD started in the middle of an episode. *The audience was cheering and applauding as The Gigglers took their position onstage for the beginning of their next number — 'Look*

Over Your Shoulder'.

13.

"If you ever need a friend," Marky sang, *"we'll be there for you."*

"Cos being there for one another," sang Ricky and Pete, "is what us Gigglers do."

"If you're feeling lost and alone," Lolly sang.

"You've got nobody, and you're far from home," sang Roxie.

"Just look over your shoulder, and we'll be there!"

⋈

Harry was clinging to Glenn's arm as they entered the auditorium. The entire theatre was packed, save for the front row.

He hadn't meant to tell about what had happened in Marky's dressing room, but spotting his dad outside the main theatre, Harry had burst into tears and ended up blurting out everything to him; about the liquor, even about the white powder on the table.

He had never seen his dad so angry before, and it frightened him.

As they took their seats in the centre of the row,

Harry couldn't help darting quick glances up at The Gigglers and Marky-Mark on the stage as they sang 'Look Over Your Shoulder'.

While Harry sat huddled up next to his dad watching the performance, he felt the knot in his stomach twisting tighter and tighter.

"*When you're at school.*"

"*Look over your shoulder!*"

"*Alone in your room.*"

 "*Look over your shoulder!*"

"Wherever you go," sang Marky, "whatever you do!" Marky suddenly looked directly at Harry and winked.

Harry froze, and then hid his face against his dad's arm.

"*Look over your shoulder... we're there for you!*"

❧

A couple of hours later, Harry and his dad were sitting in the theatre. The audience had left, and the set was being cleared.

"It's all okay now, Harry," Glenn said. "I've taken

care of it. They've gone and they sure as hell won't be coming back. No one threatens my son like that. Now, I've got a few more things to do here, so go and fetch your schoolwork from the dressing room."

Harry cringed. "Please, Dad," he implored. "Can't you come with me?"

"What?" said Glenn, exasperated. "For Christ sakes, Harry, no! Look, I told you… I took care of it. They're gone and they're not coming back. Now stop being a baby and go and get your stuff!" Seeing Harry's hurt expression, Glenn sighed. "Look, I know you've had an upsetting experience and we'll talk it over when we get home — but I have a lot of stuff to sort out and I need you to go and collect your things together, okay, buddy?"

Harry nodded, and defeated, he sloped off out of the auditorium.

Harry made his way down the hallway towards the dressing room to retrieve his coat and school bag. A few hours ago the studio was bustling with people, it was

now eerily quiet, with only a few crew members still milling about. Harry wished desperately that he could just turn and run back to the safety of the theatre, but of course he couldn't do that (*stop being a baby*); his dad would be furious.

Just then, Gavin came around the corner towards him, making Harry jump.

"Hey, Harry," said Gavin. "You okay?"

"Yeah," Harry said shakily. "I'm fine. I'm just gonna go fetch my stuff."

"Yeah. Your dad mentioned what happened earlier. Don't worry, okay? They're finished now. Between you and me… Mark, Ricky and the rest have been on thin ice the past couple of months — but this is the last straw. They'll never work again after this. Believe me."

"Yeah, thanks," said Harry, smiling weakly.

"All right, kid," he said. "You take care now."

Gavin gave Harry's shoulder a squeeze and carried on his way.

"See ya, Gavin," called Harry.

Then he paused.

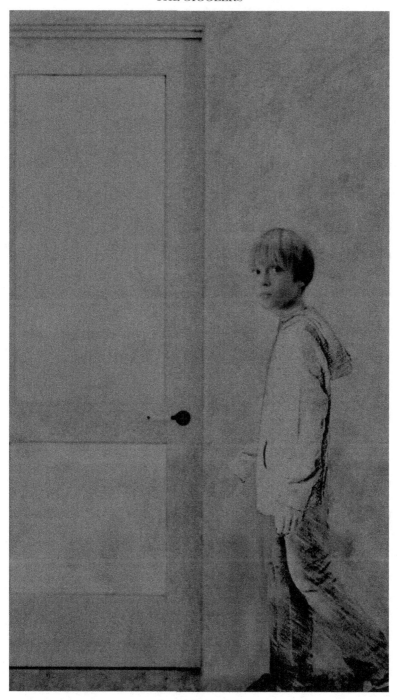

"Gavin?"

But Gavin had already gone.

Harry turned the last corner and stopped outside the dressing room where he was doing his homework earlier.

Harry cautiously turned the handle and opened the door. It was nearly pitch-black inside despite the dim light from the hallway. He frantically fumbled for the light switch and turned it on. Then, leaving the door ajar, Harry began stuffing papers and books into his backpack. He grabbed his coat and bag, turned off the light and scurried out of the room, shutting the door behind him.

Harry started walking quickly back along the corridor, when the main light was switched off, plunging the corridor into relative darkness. Running now, he turned the corner and he saw one of the crew members wearing a t-shirt with 'The Gigglers' imprinted on the back; standing outside Marky's dressing room. Relieved, Harry headed towards him. Then, the man turned around.

It was Pete.

Harry was about to run back the way he'd come, but Ricky appeared from around the corner — and between them, they dragged Harry into Marky's dressing room, where he, Lolly and Roxie were waiting.

⋈

Harry was struggling and kicking out at Pete and Ricky as they tried to keep their grip.

"Get off me," Harry yelled. "Get off... I'm warning you!"

Roxie and Lolly clutched each other in mock terror, while Marky-Mark raised an eyebrow.

"Yeah?" said Pete. "And what are you gonna do about it, huh? Huh? That's right, you're not gonna do nothing." Pete shook Harry by the shoulders. "Now *shut up...* and behave yourself." He gave Harry a sharp swat across the butt for emphasis.

"You got that?" Ricky asked.

Harry nodded.

"Good."

"That's better," Marky said with a warm smile.

"Come here, Harry." He gestured to the chair next to him. Ricky and Pete let go of Harry and he went and sat down beside him. "We're friends, aren't we?"

"Yes," said Harry.

"Now, tell me," he said, "what are the most important things that friends do?"

Harry wasn't sure how to respond.

"You don't know? Hmm… hey, let's go around the room and talk about what makes a good friend! Ricky, why don't you start?"

"Friends share with each other," said Ricky. "Lolly?"

"Friends make each other feel good," Lolly said, stroking Roxie's inner thigh. Roxie moaned and nodded in agreement.

"Pete?" said Marky.

"Friends keep secrets."

"Now," Marky said. "What do friends never do?"

"Ooh! Ooh! I know this one," said Lolly. Her tone suddenly switched to icy cold, and she stared at Harry. "Tattletale."

"I didn't," Harry said. "I swear I—"

"Li-ar, li-ar," sang Roxie.

Harry sprang up from his chair and lunged towards the door. "Please," he begged. "You've got to believe me. Whatever you guys are thinking about doing — please don't!"

Pete grabbed Harry by the arm. "We got fired because of you, you little fucker!" He twisted Harry's arm up behind his back, there was an audible crack, and Harry screamed.

"Nobody likes a tattletale, Harry," said Lolly, shaking her head.

"Oh my god." Roxie snickered, pointing at the spreading wet patch on the crotch of Harry's jeans. "He's not even potty trained!"

Harry was crying hard now, in too much pain to be embarrassed. "Please…"

"Eww!" exclaimed Ricky. "Jesus Christ! How old did you say you were again?"

"Please," said Harry between sobs. "Just stop this now. Oh god… I can't feel my arm! Please… let me go."

"I'll tell you what we're going to do," Marky said, all facade of friendliness now vanished. "We're going now, but we're going to leave you in here to think about what you did."

"No… please!"

Pete let go of his arm and Harry collapsed to the floor.

Marky, Roxie, Lolly and Ricky exited the room. Pete switched off the light before he also left — locking the door.

Harry sat against the wall in his sodden jeans, crying bitterly, and cradling his arm. Then on the other side of the door, he heard Marky-Mark: *"You're going to spend the rest of your life looking over your shoulder after this — cos rest assured, we'll be watching you."*

14.

Ricky and Pete escorted Harry onto the stage, where Lolly, Roxie and Marky sat perched on a couple of neon couches around a coffee table. Marky stood up and walked over to them. "Well, hey there, Harry. How's it goin', bud? Wow, it's been a long time!"

He gestured to where Lolly and Roxie were lounging, and Pete and Ricky walked Harry over to them. Roxie and Lolly moved apart to make room for him, and under duress, Harry sat down between them; they entwined their arms around him like vines. Ricky and Marky then sat down on the couch opposite. Only Pete remained standing.

"Look at us, all back together again!" Roxie gave Harry an affectionate cheek pinch.

Lolly smiled at him. "Just like a little family reunion, huh?"

"Yeah," murmured Harry.

"Hey," Marky said, "to celebrate, why don't we have a drink? Pete, can you grab that bottle of Vodka?"

"Sure thing, Marky!"

"I'll get the glasses," said Ricky, getting up.

Ricky and Pete exited the stage.

"So, dude," Marky said, turning to Harry. "How old are you now?"

"Twenty-one," said Harry.

"Twenty-one," Marky said. "Wow!"

"Twenty-one!" said Lolly. "So you're legal now. Cool!"

Roxie shook her head. "It seems like only yesterday you were just a cute little kid."

"And now look at you," Lolly said. "All grown up."

Harry took a deep breath, and keeping his tone calm and measured, he attempted to reason with them. "Listen, Mark, Roxanne, Lauren. I understand you have your grievances, but surely we can discuss this. We can negotiate these matters in a neutral, *legal* setting and come to a conclusion that is satisfactory for all parties concerned."

"Shut up," said Roxie, smiling.

"*Roxanne… Lauren.*" Lolly chuckled. "What's with all the formality, huh?"

"Honestly, Harry," said Marky. "We're all friends here, aren't we?"

"Yes," Harry said. "Yes, we are."

"Well then… relax!"

Ricky and Pete came back with an enormous bottle of Vodka and some shots glasses. They set them on the table and sat down. Marky began filling the glasses and passing them around so each of the Gigglers, and Harry had one.

"To friends reunited!" said Marky.

"To friends reunited!" Roxie, Lolly, Pete and Ricky cheered.

They all clinked their glasses — including Harry, and took the shots.

"Whoo-hoo," said Ricky. "Check out Harry! You're of age though, right? We don't want you getting in trouble with your dad."

"Nah," Marky said. "It's cool. It's cool. He's twenty-one now… isn't that right, Harry? He's a man now."

Pete snickered.

"Pete!" Marky admonished. "That's rude. Say, I've

got an idea. Harry, to prove your manhood to Pete, Ricky and the girls — I think you should finish the rest of this bottle in one drink. How about it?"

Harry was aghast. "You mean to drink that whole bottle in its entirety. Straight. In one drink, with no mixers?"

"No mixers," said Lolly, giggling.

"No mixers," Marky said. "You wanna prove you're a man? You're going to finish this entire bottle in one drink."

Harry tried to stand up, but Roxie and Lolly were still holding onto his arms. Pete straddled Harry, pinning him down and thrusting the bottle in his face; while Ricky walked behind the couch and yanked Harry's head back by his hair. With his other hand, Ricky pinched Harry's nose. This forced him to open his mouth and Pete started emptying the bottle down his throat.

"Atta boy, Harry," said Pete. "Down the hatch."

Lolly and Roxie were cheering and whooping as if it were a hazing ritual.

Harry was violently twisting to get away. His throat was swelling up and he felt like his brain and his nasal passage were on fire. He couldn't breathe.

Everything went black… and then he was on the floor. He could still see and hear the Gigglers cackling maniacally, but it was as though he were underwater.

"Psst… Harry. Hey, Harry," Marky whispered. "Look over your shoulder!"

With enormous effort, Harry managed to turn his head; then he saw Marky, and the knife.

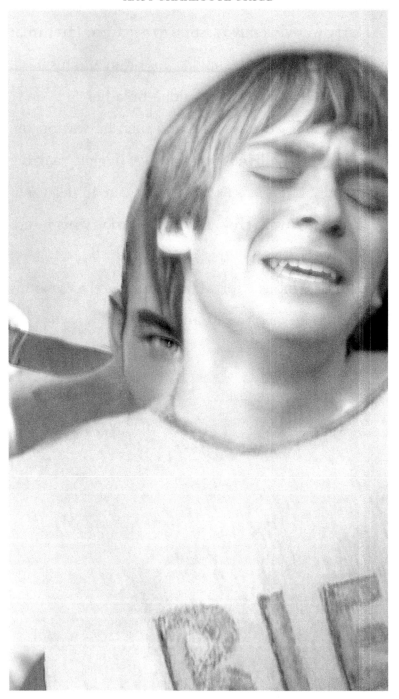

15.

Ashley sat alone in the Greenroom. The DVD had finished and the TV had gone onto standby. She was in the process of dismantling her Gigglers' stationery set, looking for something sharp. The ruler… the pencils… *then her eyes rested on The Gigglers' Study Guide.*

ъ

Ashley was sitting on her bed with her laptop propped up on a cushion on her knees. In the search bar on Facebook, she entered 'roxie lolly the gigglers'. The top result read: 'Roxie and Lolly's deLiShiOus oFFiCiOuS FaN CLuB |Join|Community|Exclusive Content|'. The profile photo showed Lolly and Roxie making sultry eyes at the camera; wearing customised/sexualised versions of their Gigglers' costumes.

Ashley clicked on the link, and then she was on their page. Excited, she scrolled down the timeline for a little bit; then she clicked on 'Photos'.

She started clicking through the behind-the-scenes pictures of their time on 'The Gigglers', 'liking' each one in turn until she reached a blurred-out image.

Across it, read 'Content unavailable. Join for access.'

Going back to the timeline, Ashley scrolled around to find a way to join. It was unclear, so she clicked on 'Message'.

After pausing for a moment, she began to type:

'Hiiii OMG!!! I was sooooooooo excited to find your Facebook page! I would LOVE to join the fan club!!!! I've been a huge fan of yours since I was 10 and I first saw The Gigglers! I own all The Gigglers' merchandise! The t-shirts, books, DVDs, action figures, mugs, stickers, the albums... including the limited edition of The Gigglers' Greatest Hits! I also used to get The Gigglers' Calendar and The Gigglers' Study Guide every year until they stopped doing them. I think you guys are sooooooooo cool and I wish wish wish I could hang out with you! Please please please message back! It would make my day! Lots and lots and lots of love from Ashley xxxxxx'

She clicked 'Send'.

Opening another window, Ashley decided to go on YouTube. After briefly checking through notifications

on the 'Glitzy Girlz' makeup tutorial channel she ran with Carla, Ashley clicked on a video in her 'recommendations'; a half-hour-long compilation of cute/funny cat videos.

A couple of little black kittens were leaping about on a sofa, synchronised to look as though they were dancing to House of Pain's 'Jump Around'. Ashley was giggling and cooing at their adorable antics when she was hit with a bunch of Facebook notifications. With a squeak of excitement, she paused the video and clicked back on the window which was still open on Roxie and Lolly's fan page.

Her face dropped. Roxie and Lolly had screenshotted her message and posted it on their page, along with the caption which they had tagged her in: 'RABID new wannabe FAN wants to join… whaddya guys think?? ;)'

The post already had fourteen 'likes', including several 'lolz'. Underneath, there was a string of nasty comments attacking Ashley on everything from her message to her appearance. Even as she stared at the hideous post, the list of 'likes' and cruel comments was

visibly mounting.

For a moment, Ashley was frozen, as her eyes filled up with tears. Eventually snapping out of her shock, she blocked Roxie and Lolly and closed the window. Shutting the laptop, she got up and placed it on her dresser. Then she laid down on her bed and started to sob in anger, shock, and humiliation. Jemima jumped up onto the bed and Ashley cuddled her, crying into her soft fur. She still couldn't quite believe what had just happened.

After a while, Ashley reached for her phone and rang Carla.

✄

Ashley had just finished tidying her hair and reapplying her eye makeup when she heard Carla's knock. "Come in!"

Carla opened the door and walked in, and Ashley got up to give her a hug.

Carla was looking at her, appalled. "Oh my god... baby, are you okay?"

Ashley shook her head and started to cry all over

again. Carla put an arm around her shoulders. "Come on, let's go sit on the bed, and tell me everything right from the beginning."

❧

Laying on Ashley's bed, they were looking at the post on Carla's account.

"So, a few minutes later I checked their page again and found this post. I just don't understand why they would do this to me… I mean all I did was write saying how much The Gigglers meant to me. Why would they… what did I do to deserve this?!"

"Nothing, sweetie," said Carla. "They're just a couple of nasty little bitches who—"

"How am I meant to re-watch my Gigglers DVDs after this? Knowing what a bunch of cretins they *really* are?"

"Don't re-watch them," Carla said quickly. "We have a *whole* new obsession, remember?" She grabbed her bag and pulled out a brand-new DVD boxset, with a flourish. "Zombie Night Season 12!!"

Ashley brightened for a moment but remained

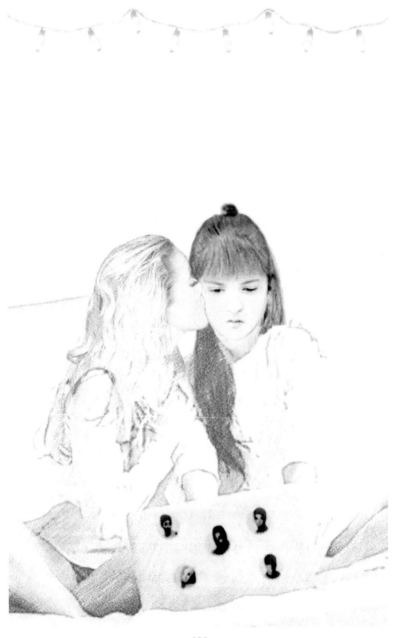

sombre.

"I guess," Carla said, "I guess you just have to… you know… separate the art from the artist. Remember that they are just *playing* these characters. They're completely different in real life. So, by disassociating them from the actors playing them — you can still carry on loving the characters as before."

"Wow," said Ashley, impressed. "You got a lot out of that 'Intro to Psychology' class! But, yeah, I know you're right. It just still… really hurts, you know?"

Carla gave Ashley another hug. "Of course it's gonna hurt, babe. That was completely fucked up what they did, and you in no way deserved it."

There was a long pause.

"Look, I…" Ashley started. "I mean tell me honestly… was there anything in my message that could be taken as even slightly offensive?"

"Well."

"Seriously."

"Well," said Carla. "Maybe what you put about them no longer making The Gigglers' calendars and

Study Guides hammered home to them that they're past it. You know… no longer relevant?"

Ashley was outraged. "But that wasn't what I meant at all!"

"*You* know that," Carla said. "And *I* know that, but… plus, haven't you heard the stuff that's going around about them now?"

"Bad stuff?"

"Oh, yeah," said Carla. "Lolly — complete alcoholic, and Roxie? Totally off the rails. Seriously, she's been in and out of rehab like three times now for… I think it was coke, molly… something like that. But they are both *major* fuck-ups. They shouldn't even have access to Facebook."

Ping!

Someone had just posted a new comment. A 'Leah Martin': 'OMFG just spat out my soda! What a looser and did you check out her profile picture? LOLOLOLOL!!!'

"Right, bitch," Carla said. "Let's check out *your* profile."

Leah Martin's profile picture showed a woman, probably in her early thirties, with a split dyed fringe, an enormous shovel-like jaw, and a frozen sneer. She described herself as being an 'actress', a 'stand-up comedian', and also as the owner of an Etsy store that designed outfits for dogs.

"Hitler liked dogs too," said Ashley with a contemptuous sniff.

"Stupid bitch," Carla scoffed.

Clicking back to Lolly and Roxie's page, Carla began to type out a reply: 'Learn to spell, asshole!' But before she clicked 'Send', Ashley stopped her. "No, wait! I've got a better idea."

She typed their blog name into the search bar and hit 'enter'. *Ashley started to make a new blog entry — titled 'Lolly & Roxie: The Jump N' Jive Junkies'; and cackling with laughter, Ashley and Carla set to work on it.*

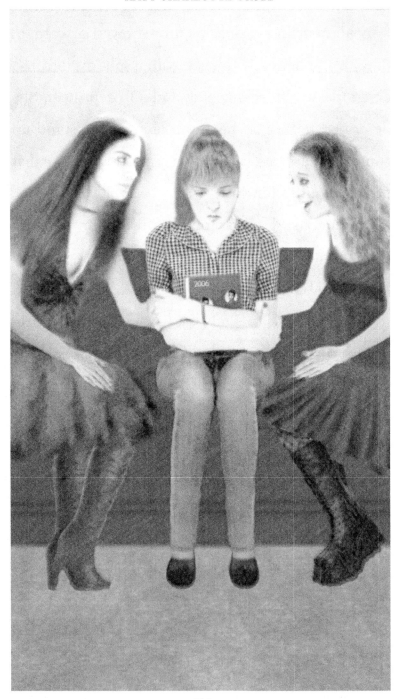

16.

After putting the contents of her stationery set back in the case, Ashley had just tucked a pencil under her back bra-strap when Lolly and Roxie came in.

"Heyy," said Lolly. "Whatcha doin'?"

Ashley nearly jumped out of her skin. "Uh, nothing," she said, trying to appear nonchalant. "I'm just…"

"Checking out your new Gigglers' Stationery set?" asked Roxie. "Pretty cool, huh?"

"Yeah," Ashley said warily. "It's great."

"And," said Lolly. "What do you think of your Gigglers' Study Guide?"

Ashley looked down at it. The date on the cover was 2006. "Neat."

"Yeah," Roxie said, "Lolly and I thought you'd like that!"

They sat down either side of Ashley, and Lolly reached out her hand onto Ashley's thigh. Ashley shifted away from her into the centre of the couch, but Lolly and Roxie just moved in closer; hemming her in between them.

"We just wanted to check that you were okay," said Lolly. "Are you feeling lonely? Are you missing Carla?" She took Carla's friendship bracelet out of her skirt pocket and waved it in front of Ashley's face. Ashley made a grab for it, but Lolly just batted her hand away; flipping the bracelet to Roxie, who caught it in her fist.

"Don't worry," Roxie said. "You'll be seeing her soon. And in the meantime, your pals Roxie and Lolly will keep you company!" Roxie glided a hand down Ashley's arm. "This blouse is so cute on you."

Lolly began to massage her shoulders; Ashley let out a tiny involuntary whimper as she felt Lolly's fingertips moving down and around her shoulder blades, closer and closer to where the pencil sat lodged beneath her bra-strap.

Lolly paused. "You feel really tense, hon," she said. "Sure you're okay?"

Ashley nodded.

"She's being awfully quiet," commented Roxie. She smiled at Ashley. "You're not feeling shy with us, are you?"

"No," Ashley squeaked.

"No?" said Roxie, sweeping aside Ashley's heavy fringe.

They were both peering into her face now, grinning like cats at a mousehole.

Ashley cringed and cowered away from them, shuffling back into the couch cushions. She squeezed her eyes tight shut, willing desperately for them to go away, to just leave her alone...

Suddenly, Marky's voice came through the PA: "Hey, guys, we're ready now for you to bring Ashley to the stage."

Abruptly, Lolly and Roxie got up from the couch and yanked Ashley to her feet. As they moved through the doorway, Roxie bent close to Ashley's ear. "Don't think about doing anything stupid. Trust me, it won't end well for you, honey."

Onstage, Pete and Ricky were in the process of binding Ashley to an old Bentwood chair with a couple of rolls of gaffer tape.

"Well," said Pete, as he secured Ashley's ankles to the chair legs, "at least this'll make a good one for the blog, right?" Pete cut the end of the tape, and then, satisfied that Ashley couldn't move, he and Ricky went to join Marky, Roxie and Lolly at the front of the stage.

"Now," Marky said, "before we get to know our final guest, Ashley, I think it's time for... some 'Rock N' Roll Party'!"

As the intro for 'Rock N' Roll Party' came on, The Gigglers all got into position for the number.

"When you're feeling blue," sang Marky. "When you're feeling down! We'll take you to a place where fun is all around, at the Gigglers' rock n' roll party!"

Strong though the gaffer tape was, as Ashley shifted around, she could feel it begin to stretch and slacken. With just a bit more give...

✂

"We're gonna rock, we're gonna roll," sang The Gigglers. "We're gonna rock, we're gonna roll! Cos the Gigglers' party is off the wall!"

✂

Twisting and squirming, Ashley managed to free her arms. She then set about unwrapping the tape around her ankles.

☙

"The drinks are flowing," Marky sang. "The music is too! All your friends are here waiting just for you, at the Gigglers' rock n' roll party!"

☙

Freeing herself from the gaffer tape, Ashley bolted up out of the chair and began to run.

☙

She was racing towards the wings when Roxie spotted her.

"Oh, I don't think so," said Roxie. Waiting for Ashley to run past, she reached out and caught hold of her by the wrist; Ashley screamed, and then taking the pencil, she stabbed the sharpened lead point into Roxie's arm. "Oh, fuck me!" howled Roxie, instantly letting go.

"That's for the Facebook post," Ashley told her, kicking Roxie in the shin for good measure.

Lolly ran at Ashley and grabbed her by the shoulders, but Ashley was ready for her: "This is for Carla," said Ashley, as she slammed her knee into Lolly's crotch. Lolly crumpled to the floor, groaning and clutching at her groin; but there was no time to gloat.

Ricky, Pete and Marky were running over, Pete wielding his mallet, Ricky and Marky gripping iron bars they'd hastily retrieved from the wings; so, thinking on her feet, Ashley got behind a large piece of the set wall and shoved it as hard as she could towards them — it was on wheels, and before they had time to jump out the way, it trundled straight into them.

"Take that, you fuckers!" Ashley yelled at them, before turning on her heels and running offstage.

17.

At the end of the corridor, Ashley saw what looked like an exterior door. She ran to it and was about to press down on the crash bar, when Roxie jumped out from around the corner and seized her from behind, holding her tightly. Ashley struggled violently, trying to break out of Roxie's grasp.

"*No*—" Ashley started, but Roxie clapped a hand over her mouth, cutting off her scream.

"Hey," soothed Roxie. "Hey, Ashley… *Shh!* I'm not gonna hurt you."

Ashley continued to struggle as Roxie began to manoeuvre her down the corridor to a door.

"Calm down," Roxie said. "Come on now. Relax. Walk. That's it."

Roxie took her hand away to open the door. It took her a moment as the doorknob was rickety and at first it wouldn't turn. Ashley took a big gulping breath, then Roxie, having now opened the door, pushed Ashley inside and shut the door behind them.

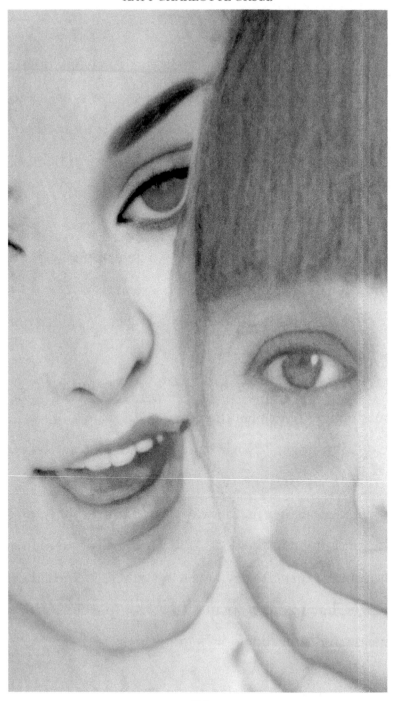

The room was sparse apart from some clothes rails with a few costumes hanging up. There was a tired-looking wooden coffee table, and in the corner was an old couch that had seen better days.

"What's the matter?" said Roxie. "Oh, you're so upset, poor thing."

She turned Ashley by the shoulder and faced her squarely. Roxie's eyes were dancing wildly. "I know," said Roxie, "this has been really really scary. And you don't deserve this. Not you. Do you?"

"N-no…" Ashley stammered.

"Are you a bad person?"

"No," said Ashley.

"That's what I thought." Roxie smiled. "I'm not either."

"No," said Ashley slowly. "You're not."

"You know that, right?"

Suddenly, all the advice from Carla and Harry solidified, and Ashley's survival instinct kicked in. "Yes," she said. "Yes, Roxie."

"I'm not gonna hurt you," said Roxie. "I would

never! And you wouldn't do anything to hurt me, right?"

"No. Of course not."

"You wouldn't."

"No," said Ashley, eyeing the bloodstained cloth tied around Roxie's wrist. "No, I wouldn't. Please——"

"*Why* are you lying to me?!" Roxie yelled.

Ashley flinched but tried not to show it. Without taking her eyes off of Roxie, or betraying her fear, she tried to make sense of the madwoman inches from her face. "I'm sorry," said Ashley, "if I hurt you…"

"Why'd you do it? Huh?"

"I… I didn't mean to," Ashley said, her tone dropping almost to a whisper. "I was just upset… I was… I was angry at you."

Roxie was genuinely caught off guard. "*What? Why?*"

Before Ashley could begin, Roxie seemed to remember herself again; her rage and her power trip. She pointed to the couch. "Sit the fuck down."

Ashley obliged, nodding at Roxie as she backed

down into the seat. Careful not to let Roxie's scattered brain dictate the direction of the conversation, Ashley persisted. "I was mad because... Because I was... I went on yours and Lolly's Facebook page, and I wrote... I messaged you about how I was a big fan of the show. And you... you and Lolly were really mean to me. You know... that post you made really hurt my feelings!"

"Bullshit," snapped Roxie. "Liar. Lie down, liar. I said *lie down*. You've been running around all night."

Ashley remained sitting upright on the couch, as Roxie sat down next to her, intimidatingly close.

"But you did, Roxie," Ashley continued. "You called me a 'rabid wannabe fan'."

Roxie snorted. She began giggling, almost flirtatiously.

"And then," said Ashley, "that mean, lousy, horrible, *hateful* follower on your page... Leah Martin... called me a loser and made fun of my profile picture." The words, the image, were still very visceral to Ashley, and she began to tear up; genuinely reliving the experience.

"Oh, boo-fucking-hoo," Roxie sneered. "Cry me a bloody river. You *excoriated* Lolly and me. We are *celebrities*. We're public figures. My reputation is *everything!*"

"Well," said Ashley. "What you said about me was public too! I mean it was on your Facebook page where everybody could see—"

"Oh, nobody's looking at *your* page," Roxie said. "Nobody cares about you. You made us look like assholes!"

Suddenly, Roxie leaned in and grabbed Ashley by the ponytail.

"Stop," cried Ashley, wincing in pain.

"You think it's *okay?*" Roxie hissed. "To call me a slut? And Lolly a drunk? You know nothing about my life!" She punctuated this with vicious yanks on Ashley's ponytail.

"Our Father," said Ashley, fighting back tears. "Who art in Heaven, hallowed be thy name…"

"Stop it!" Roxie screeched, nearly hitting the roof. "Stop *praying!*"

But Ashley did not, and Roxie let her go briefly to cover her own ears. She was momentarily overcome with some kind of emotion, and shuddered out something like a sob, before collecting herself and pointing her vitriol at Ashley once again. "You think you're so much better than me, don't you?"

"No," said Ashley. "No, of course I don't. I mean I can't imagine what it must have been like... having people watching you all the time, and being... I'm really sorry."

"You should be sorry," Roxie said, as she released her grasp and started combing Ashley's hair back into place with her fingers.

"I *am* sorry, Roxie. I'm not a mean person! I was just... angry, I guess. I shouldn't have done it. I'm really sorry."

"Then why did you? Why me? You were obsessed with me, I know. Did you wanna be like... my friend, or something?"

"I guess," Ashley said. "I mean, you guys always looked like you were having so much fun on the show...

and—"

"What's that supposed to mean?"

"Nothing," said Ashley. "Just that you seemed like you'd be fun to be friends with. I just... I don't know!"

"Well, Ashley..."

Roxie stood up and leaned over her menacingly. Ashley was beginning to lose her composure, and her patience for this game. She refused to make eye contact but quietly implored Roxie. "Let me go... Please... Please let me go. I've got people who love me! I've got family! I've got friends! God, just please. I'm eighteen, I don't wanna die!" Ashley started to cry. "Oh god... I just want to see my family again. I just want my *mum!*"

"Oh, yeah?" said Roxie. "Well, guess what. I don't have any family. I never did. All I had, was *this.*" She pointed to her face, which looked deranged in falling makeup. "I should just kill you right now. I've got nothing else to lose... I mean look at us! Tell me, Ashley. What have I got? Friends?"

"Umm... sure you do!" Ashley said. "I mean everyone has friends. I mean, Lolly. She's your friend,

isn't she?"

"She's a bitch."

"Really?"

"Oh, yeah," Roxie said. "I've wasted my whole adult life on that bitch, actually."

"Oh… wow… that's… Why do you stay friends with her then?"

"I don't know," said Roxie. She paused. "*Why?* Do you like her better than me?"

"No," Ashley said. "Besides, she was the one that was really horrible to me on Facebook."

"Yeah," said Roxie. "She's *always* that one. She was the one that made me think that you were… you know? She brainwashed me!"

"Yeah," Ashley said. "I know what you mean… Um. And again, I'm really really sorry about the blog post — really, I am! Yeah, and if you let me go, you… can share my family!"

"Really?"

"*Yes,*" said Ashley. "Honest to god!"

Roxie gave Ashley a shake. She was snapping again.

"You're full of shit! I could never share your family —
what are you talking about? You're just trying to trip
me up, aren't you?"

"No!" Ashley said. "No, I wouldn't do that! I'm not
like that." Ashley paused for a moment. "Look. I'm
sorry I did that, but what do you want? How can I
make it up to you—"

"I don't fucking *know*," said Roxie, genuinely,
desperately, searching for an answer. "*You* have to think
of that… You have to come up with that. I don't know!
See, I mean… what do I know? I'm just a… what was
it? Alcoholic, addict, slut… right? Has-been, washed-
up…"

"Look!" said Ashley. "I was wrong to say that!
Have you never made a mistake? Have you never
done anything when *you're* angry?" She stopped and
recalibrated. "Hey, Roxie? I've got an idea! Why don't
we just… before they come… before they find us…
why don't we just walk out of here right now, and we
can discuss it over… ice cream!"

Roxie let out a shrill laugh.

"Right?" Ashley said. "We can do that, right?"

"You are *something else*, aren't you?" said Roxie, chuckling. Then suddenly she clasped at her temple and shuddered. "I need a fix! I need a fucking fix!"

"A fix of what?" asked Ashley nervously.

"I don't know," Roxie said. "Coke… smack… something!" She laughed. "Blood!"

"That's funny," said Ashley with a forced giggle.

Roxie put an arm around Ashley's shoulders. Tenderly, almost romantically. "I stopped you," she said. "Actually, I stopped you because I wanted to take care of you myself."

"Take care of me in a 'murder' way… or a—"

"Yeah, in a *murder* way. To just… shut you up, so you don't go spouting off about everything that's wrong with me like *you'd* know anything about it. You know I took care of myself since I was like, thirteen years old?"

"Yeah," said Ashley. "That must have been… I can't even imagine."

"Yeah. Well, imagine it!"

"Well," Ashley said. "Talk to me about it. Tell me

what that was like… tell—"

"It was fucking hard," said Roxie. "That's what it was like! I had to grow up like… you know. I grew up on that fucking set. I-I was the only girl on that show before they cast Lolly. On that whole set besides Gin-breath Jenna. I grew up on that… I… I…"

Roxie paused, and her face displayed a rainbow of intense emotions, including panic.

18.

Standing next to Ricky and Pete, chatting with Kelsey and Finn, who had been guests on that day's show; fourteen-year-old Roxie was aware of *Jeffrey* the photographer, hovering a few feet away from her. She could always smell when he was around, sometimes even at home; his lingering, phantom stench of stale sweat, thinly masked by Armani Eau Pour Homme.

The first time; she had gone to kiss his cheek and at the last second, he turned his head, so she had wound up kissing him on the lips. Her first instinct was to recoil, but he had just laughed, and with Jenna nearby, and the crew hustling around, Roxie had laughed it off too.

Jenna was coming over to them now.

"Roxie, Pete, Ricky. Come on, kids! You all need to be onstage *soon*." She then went to where Marky was sitting; signing album covers and posters, and greeting his young fans. "Mark! Come on, honey!"

Saying goodbye to Kelsey and Finn before they were led away, Roxie turned to see Jeffrey, who was now

standing directly behind her. He winked at her, and then, under the guise of ushering her along, he slapped her on the behind. She blushed but didn't react.

"*Roxie*," Jenna called impatiently. "Come on!"

As Roxie turned to leave, Jeffrey grabbed her by the wrist as though to pull her in, and then quickly let go. It was one of his little pranks.

Slumping out of the room, Roxie ran to catch up with the others.

⋈

"*I didn't know that,*" said Ashley.

"Well," Roxie said. "Now you know."

"Yeah."

"Whatever," said Roxie. "Boys will be boys, right?"

"Um… No." Ashley faltered. She didn't agree with this but didn't know how to respond. "I… well…"

"Do you know what it's like," said Roxie, "when *everyone*. And I mean *everyone*, wants to fuck you, Ashley?"

"No," Ashley said. "I don't, Roxie."

"It's kind of a high, actually. But you'd know that, right?"

"Probably not on the scale that you've experienced it, no."

"Well," said Roxie, "on what *scale* do you know? Tell me, Ashley."

"Um…" Ashley said. "Well, there was this creep at school, Evan, and he wanted to go out with me. Anyway, we went back to my house, and he really wanted to have sex with me, and I didn't want to. Then the next day he was telling everybody that I was the one pestering *him* for sex. It was horrible, and Carla was the only one that stood by me. And that's… that's the kind of friend she is." Ashley stopped and looked at Roxie, pleading. "Please… please, you've got to tell me… You guys haven't…? Where *is* she?"

Roxie smirked. "I don't know what happened to Carla. But… I assume it wasn't very good. We have uh… Pete. He's got a little bit of a violent temper. Ya know? He just got out of the can… He was in there almost a year."

"About the arson?"

"Yeah," said Roxie. "That."

"Look," Ashley said. "I'm really sorry, but we seriously need to get out of here! Look… can we just… can we just go? Please, I'm *begging* you!"

Roxie leaned in towards her, eyes glittering. "Well… beg me more. Show me that you mean it." She pointed to the carpet. "In fact… I think you should get on your knees."

Ashley hesitated.

"*Get* on your knees."

Ashley stood up from the couch and then, trembling with shame, she knelt before Roxie. "Please," Ashley began, her voice barely audible. "Please…?" Then, suddenly she broke and began to plead with Roxie in earnest. "Please, just let us just *get out of here*! Please!"

"But it's so nice and cosy in here," purred Roxie.

"What do you… what do you *want* from me?"

"I want from you…" Roxie mused. "I want the same thing from you, that everybody wants from me. Do you know what that is?"

"No," said Ashley.

"I want you to get back up here." Roxie indicated to

the couch. "I want you to lie down and shut the fuck up. And enjoy it."

"If I do," Ashley said. "Will you let me go?"

Roxie reached down and ruffled Ashley's fringe. "Depends how good you are."

"Okay," said Ashley, slowly getting to her feet. "All right." Roxie stood up and Ashley lay down on the couch, her head leant against the armrest. She bent her legs back to make room for Roxie. "Like this?"

"Yeah," said Roxie, sitting down. "That's good." She paused. "I'm gonna sing you a little song. What's your favourite song?"

Ashley didn't answer.

"You know all the songs, don't you?"

"Um..." said Ashley. "I like... I like 'Look Over Your Shoulder' because it's about friends being there for each other."

"Hmm... exactly! Mmm... okay—"

"And that's all you're gonna do, right?"

"I don't know," said Roxie. "I don't trust you. You *betrayed* me. Blouse. Off. Now!"

"Okay," Ashley said, and, sitting up slightly, she began awkwardly removing her blouse, while Roxie looked on deliriously. In a strange, almost childish move, she put an arm around Ashley and rested her head on her chest.

Closing her eyes, Roxie began to sing: "If you're feeling lost and alone. You've got nobody and you're far from home. Just look over your shoulder and I'll be there." As she crooned, her hand wandered down towards Ashley's breast.

"What are you… what are you doing?" asked Ashley.

With that, Roxie bolted upright, and then to her feet, reclaiming her dominance. "What's in your hair?" she demanded. "*Contraband?* Take it out. Hair down, now!"

"All right," said Ashley, undoing the scrunchie and shaking her hair loose.

"Now stand up."

"Okay."

"Okay, now drop your trousers and panties—"

"No!" Ashley protested. "Please… this is so *humiliating*

and messed up and… No!"

"You humiliated *me!*" Roxie shot back. "Me and Lolly! So, *drop your trousers and panties* and spread your legs nice and wide for me. Bending over the arm of the couch."

Ashley began unbuttoning the fly on her jeans. It took her a moment as her hands were shaking. Burning with intense embarrassment, she slid down her jeans and panties with one hand while trying to cover herself with the other.

"Now step out of them, and *bend over* like I said." Roxie stared at Ashley, who was now standing motionless with her jeans and panties around her ankles. "I'm not going to ask again."

Wordlessly, Ashley did as she was told. Spreading her legs shoulder-width apart, she bent over; her face pressed against the worn, cracked, leather upholstery, her arms dangling loosely over the side.

"Wider," said Roxie, giving Ashley's thigh a slap. *With a muted whimper, Ashley moved her feet further apart. "Good girl."*

"Like this?" asked Roxie, her voice barely above a whisper. *Sitting on the vinyl sheet, legs spread apart, she leant in towards the camera lens.*

"Yeah," said Jeffrey. "Just like that. You know, Roxie… you're a very pretty little girl. Have you got a boyfriend?"

Suddenly, Jenna knocked on the door and opened it. Roxie and Jeffrey looked up. "Come on, Roxie! You and the other kids have to be onstage in five minutes." She looked at Jeffrey. "Five minutes, okay, Jeffrey?"

"No worries," Jeffrey said. "We're just about finished here."

"Well, Roxie?" said Jenna. Roxie got up, and smoothing down her skirt, she walked over to Jenna's side. "*And*, what do you say to Jeffrey?"

"Thank you."

"No problem." He smiled. "Always a pleasure. Great shots today, sweetie."

As Jenna walked out into the corridor and Roxie went to follow her, Jeffrey smirked and gave her a wave.

eyes closed, and Roxie began to kiss her passionately while stroking Ashley's face and hair.

As the kiss came to a close, Roxie's mood shifted yet again. She sat up next to Ashley and gave her shoulder a shake. "Ash-ley… look at meee! *Come on!* Sit up and look at me."

"Okay." Ashley sniffled. She opened her eyes and gingerly pulled herself upright, wincing in pain.

"Now," said Roxie, getting up from the couch. "Tell me what you see." Her tone was still playful, but there was now a slight edge to it.

"Um… you?" Ashley said, bewildered.

"Mmm-hmm…?"

"I don't know what…" said Ashley. "I don't know what you want me to *say*."

"I want you to describe what you see right now."

Ashley looked at Roxie, doing a silent inventory of her appearance; taking in her tangle of blonde corkscrew curls and heart-shaped lips smeared with scarlet lipstick. Her large, brown, upturned eyes were a mess of smudged black eyeshadow and eyeliner.

"Umm…" Ashley began. "You're very beautiful. And—"

"Do you know," said Roxie, "how many people would *kill* to be you right now?"

"Yeah… uh—"

"Relax."

Ashley whimpered. "You've got beautiful eyes. They've got a real mani…" Ashley quickly corrected herself. "*Expressive* quality to them!"

"Go on," said Roxie.

"Your eye makeup's on point. Your hair's beautiful… do you use mousse?"

"Spray," Roxie said. "And a little backcombing actually."

"I love it!" said Ashley. "You know what? When we get out of here… you know, cos me and… well, Carla and I do makeup tutorials on YouTube — but maybe *we* could do one together. To show a different side of you, away from all this… Gigglers' stuff. D'you think?"

"What are you, my publicist now?" Roxie snapped.

"No, no, no… just—"

"Well, what would you do? Believe me, I've been in the business for fifteen years and I've had a lot of people do my makeup… and a lot of people do my hair."

"No, no," Ashley said. "I love it, I love it! I wasn't saying… anything like that. I was just saying that we do a YouTube tutorial on how to create your look. You think?"

"Hmm…"

"Come on," said Ashley cajolingly. "Don't tell me that doesn't sound like fun!" She paused. "Also, is it okay if I get dressed again? I'm a little cold."

"Hmm… Fine. But, just your blouse and panties."

Gratefully, Ashley bent down to retrieve her clothes from where they lay in a little heap beside the couch; and then, under Roxie's scrutinous gaze, she pulled her panties back on and slipped her arms into the sleeves of the blouse.

"Do you really think," said Roxie, as Ashley buttoned her blouse, "that people are still interested in the way I do my makeup? *Honestly?*"

"Absolutely!" Ashley assured her.

"Really?"

"Yeah! I mean your whole look is very Britney… But," said Ashley, standing up, "you know maybe a better place for us to talk about this is if we make a run for it and—"

Roxie cut her off. "Stop talking about running, *okay*? I've let you put your clothes back on. And I'm willing to hear what you have to say. I'm willing to listen about the makeup shit because it seems like you know what you're doing… *But*, if you keep talking about running out of here — this isn't gonna end well."

"Okay," Ashley said. "No running… no running!"

"Why do you wanna run out of here so badly anyway? Don't you like spending time with me?"

"I do," said Ashley. "But I'm also really conscious about Lolly, Marky, Pete and Ricky bursting through the door and—"

"Why! Who cares about them? They're all idiots anyway. Really, they are. All idiots. Why? Did you have a favourite?"

"Well," said Ashley. "Not apart from you."

"Oh, come on. You don't need to say that just for my ego! Who was your favourite?"

"You were," Ashley said. "Honestly."

"Fine then, your next favourite?"

"Well." Ashley pondered. "Probably Lolly. I mean, you know, being girls... like I tried to... it's kind of embarrassing now, but... I tried to copy your hair and makeup — like when I was at school."

"Who?" Roxie said. "Mine? Or hers?"

"Umm... to be honest, I liked yours the best. You know with your whole Britney/Suicide Girl thing going on."

"You like that?"

"I love that!"

"What did you think of hers?"

"I like hers too," Ashley said. "I just—"

"You do?"

"Yeah..."

"I think she's a sanctimonious little bitch," said Roxie conspiratorially.

"Yeah."

"*What?*"

Ashley recognised that Roxie had switched personalities again and that bad-mouthing Lolly (albeit unwittingly) was clearly a bridge too far. "I meant…" Ashley said, attempting to walk back the remark. "I meant 'Yeah?' Like, because you know… I don't know. I don't know anything about you. Or *her*. Really."

"She's a control freak," said Roxie. "She always wants to control me."

"Oh, Roxie," Ashley said. "But you're far too strong to let anyone…"

Roxie sat back down, and Ashley sat too; on the floor, leaning against the couch. "I'm *not* strong. I'm *weak*. I'm a junkie. Lolly, she… she's the strong one."

Ashley, unsure of where this was going, decided just to let it go, to just *keep* Roxie talking.

"She's so strong," said Roxie. "They all *broke* me. Not like they got me *whole*, ya know? They all just *want to take my magic white light* and put it into a little box to make *money* off of! And they did it till they broke me,

and then they broke me *good*. Lolly's the only person I could ever trust…"

"It's good to have friends."

"She keeps me honest," Roxie said. "Keeps me on the straight n' narrow, ya know? I'm real lucky to have her…"

"And she's lucky to have you," said Ashley, tentatively patting Roxie's leg.

Roxie was getting weepy. "I'm so lucky… Never got lucky with money, never was lucky in health, but, I have been lucky in love…"

Ashley frowned. "Well," she said. "That's, that sounds just *lovely*."

"She is *also* in recovery," said Roxie. "Makes sure I go to my meetings. Holds onto my drugs for me. Makes sure I don't overdo it. Cos if it was up to me? Pffft. I'd be dead by now."

"So," Ashley said uncertainly. "She, uh, *drugs* you?"

Roxie stood up and stared at Ashley accusingly. "Anyone ever told you, you have a big mouth?"

"Do you mean like physically… or…?"

"As in you talk a lot," said Roxie. "You say a lot. You talk a lot of shit. And you seem to think you're better than everyone. And that you *know* more than everyone."

"Umm…"

"*Do you?*" Roxie demanded.

"No."

"So why do you say things like that?"

"Well," said Ashley. "I'm kinda nervous… and I just start talking… and, I'm just gonna shut up now, okay?"

"I think that's a good idea," Roxie said. "Yeah. Shut your mouth or I'll shut it for you." Roxie grabbed hold of Ashley's head and thrust it under her skirt, pulling it towards her crotch.

And that's where they were when the door shoved open.

20.

Roxie immediately let go of Ashley and looked at her, scared and sheepish, like a little girl caught being naughty.

"Ooh... what's this here?" said Lolly. "A party?"

Ashley and Roxie looked up; Ashley in terror, and Roxie with a quickly composed posture of mean-girl cool.

"Hey, baby," Roxie said, walking over. She leaned in to hug Lolly, but Lolly was agitated and rejected the embrace.

"So, what have you been doing in here?"

"She's just been... making amends," said Roxie.

"Oh, yeah?"

"She's a whiny little bitch though. I had to teach her a lesson. A little... humility."

Roxie turned to look down at Ashley, who was shifting around, trying to get into a more comfortable position. "Oh, I'm sorry," said Roxie. "Did I say you could move? Sit *down!*"

"I was just—" Ashley started.

"You heard the woman," said Lolly, even more aggressive for her lack of emotion.

Ashley nodded and sat back down on the floor at the side of the couch; leaning against the armrest. She bowed her head in a show of submission and repentance.

Roxie turned back to Lolly. "Oh my god," she whispered. "You got here just in time. I am *crashing so hard*."

"Again?" said Lolly with an exaggerated sigh. "Seriously?"

Roxie pressed her palms together and brought them to her mouth — '*please!*'. She took Lolly's hand and kissed up her arm, grovelling.

Lolly shook her head. "I don't think I have anything left, babe."

"Wait, *what?*" said Roxie, panicking.

Lolly shrugged, and watched, cool as a cucumber, as Roxie rapidly became unglued.

After a second, she reached into her pocket and tossed a little baggie of heroin at Roxie, laughing a

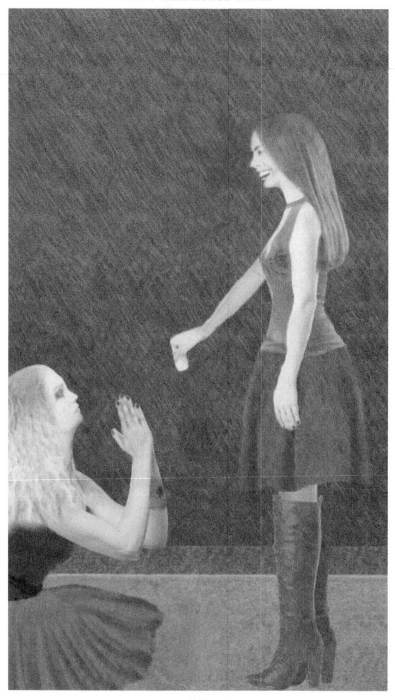

little too hard at the prank; another sick little game the two of them played pretty much daily.

"You are such a freak!" Lolly cried.

Roxie picked up the bag and tried to tear it open, but her hands were trembling too hard.

"Give me that, silly," said Lolly. She grabbed the bag back from an acquiescent Roxie and sat on the couch, with Roxie quickly following at her feet, on the floor, prepared for the ritual.

Lolly proceeded to cut the drugs into lines on the surface of the coffee table as Roxie looked on in silence. She rolled up a dollar bill and held it up for Roxie to use.

"Thank you," Roxie said softly, piously.

Lolly simply nodded. Roxie leant down and hoovered up the drugs in one swoop, frantically, blowing it around in the process.

"*Hey*," yelled Lolly. She grabbed Roxie by the shoulder and gave her a shove. "You're gonna *waste* it! What the hell?"

"What... gives?" Roxie said, already impaired.

"Are you *deranged?*" Lolly smacked Roxie on the head. Roxie groaned and then glared at her.

"I'm just *trying* to get un-sick!"

"Wow," said Lolly. "I can't even look at you. Like, it's actually painful."

"Someone's in a mood," Roxie said flippantly.

"Mystifying, isn't it? Why would I be in a mood, having to clean up after your ass all the time, *hmmm!* Give me *that*," she said, snatching the bill. "God, you're sloppy." Using the bill, Lolly tried to shove the powder back into a little pile, exaggerating the motion and her effort, glancing at Roxie occasionally to make sure she was watching.

And she was, moping but resigned.

"I'm so sick of all this," said Roxie.

"Well. That makes two of us."

"You know?" Roxie said. "You're a real bitch, Lauren." Her eyes were at half-mast, the drugs were acting as a temporary truth serum. It was unacceptable to Lolly, who smacked her again and seethed.

"I'm a bitch? All I do is clean up after you!"

"Oh, yeah," said Roxie. "You're a real saint. Keeping me doped up in your sick little cage."

"You built your own cage, Roxanne," Lolly said, her voice dropping to a frightening whisper. "And mine too. And I know you leaked that fucking sex tape! Don't even bother denying it. I *know* it was you! What the fuck was going through your head?"

⋈

Grabbing her jeans, Ashley began to pull herself along the carpet towards the door, which Lolly had left slightly ajar. Making sure to keep her head down, sticking close to the wall, Ashley moved along inch by inch; freezing every couple of seconds to make sure they hadn't spotted her. It was as though she were playing a lethal version of 'Red Light, Green Light'.

Finally reaching the door, Ashley slid her hand into the crack between the door and the frame, and praying it wouldn't creak, she pulled it open; just wide enough that she would be able to crawl through. She paused (*Red Light*), and without daring to turn around, she listened to Roxie and Lolly for a moment — they were

having what sounded like a pretty heated argument. Then Lolly shouted at Roxie, and Ashley heard a slap, (*Green Light*); using this as a cover she slipped out of the room.

Once in the corridor, Ashley continued to crawl for another couple of metres before getting silently to her feet. She'd left her shoes behind so at least she didn't have to worry about her soles squeaking. Looking around the corner at the fire exit door, she was just summoning up the courage to make a run for it when the door swung open with a loud clang. It was Ricky, and he was carrying three giant rolls of Bubble Wrap — he showed no sign of having seen her, so Ashley tiptoed back along the way she had come. Past the costume room, from which (mercifully) she could still hear Roxie and Lolly fighting, were two more doors; one with a light shining underneath. She slinked towards it.

Stopping outside, she peered through the crack in the hinges. Pete was in there, finishing a phone call. On the table in the corner of the room was a pile of

bags and jackets. Ashley watched Pete carefully as he put the iPhone into the left-side pocket of a brown leather sling bag, sitting on the edge of the table. She decided to go and hide in the next room while she waited for him to leave.

෧

"I'm sorry, baby," Roxie said. The adrenaline had sobered her up a little. She was quiet for a moment and then she looked over at Lolly. "It was *Ashley*. She's been dripping all kinds of poison in my ear… what was that she called you again? Oh, yeah. A sanctimonious little bitch."

"*Excuse me?*" said Lolly. "What the fuck? *Ashley*, is that true?"

They both looked over the arm of the couch at the spot where Ashley had been sitting. Simultaneously mouthing '*what the fuck*', they suddenly whirled around to see the door was open.

"Devious little bitch," Roxie said, almost impressed.

"Come on." Lolly reached out a hand to Roxie. "Let's go find her."

Ashley was doing up her jeans when Roxie and Lolly entered the room.

"There you are!" Lolly said, laughing. "Where do you think you're going, huh?"

"Nowhere…" said Ashley.

"You're such a little liar," Roxie said. She turned to Lolly. "You know she was talking about running out, the whole time we were in there?"

"I swear!" said Ashley. "It just seemed like you both needed some privacy and…"

"You're so full of shit," Roxie said. "I know exactly what you were trying to do. You were gonna try and run out of here so you could betray us all over again."

"God, no! Like I said, I—"

"Bullshit," said Roxie. "She's such a fucking liar."

Lolly moved forward until she was inches away from Ashley's face. "So, tell me, Ashley. Tell me what you were saying about me back there. Believe me, I'll get it out of you one way or another."

"I… I—" Ashley took a sidestep towards the door.

"Make another move and you're dead," said Roxie quickly.

Ashley dropped her hands to her sides and froze.

"Right," said Lolly. "I'm gonna ask you for the last fucking time, *what* did you call me?"

"I'm *telling* you," Ashley said. "I didn't say anything about you!"

"And you expect me to believe that. After your diatribe about us on your trashy little blog?"

Ashley stared at Lolly for a few seconds, shaking. "You wanna talk about *trashy?*" she said. "You guys *are* trash! You know, if you hadn't been *so* nasty to me on Facebook, I would never have even *thought* of writing that blog post."

"*Oh, please!*" said Lolly. "All we did was call it like we saw it."

"*Yeah,*" Ashley retorted. "So did I! Did it ever occur to you, that if you guys didn't act like snotty, entitled bitches, then people wouldn't have so much fodder to write about you? It's all such a desperate ploy to remain in the limelight. *God,* by the look of your IMDb pages

the last time you guys were relevant was nearly eight years ago! You're pathetic!"

This struck a nerve with Roxie and Lolly.

"Right," said Roxie. "I've had enough of *listening* to her mouth. It's time to shut her *the fuck* up. Let's kill her right here."

"Easy," Lolly said out of the side of her mouth. "We promised Pete. And they're all setting up. But, I think we can kill some time…"

"That trash-mouth," said Roxie. "It does have *other uses*. How about it? As my gift to you. A way of apologising for before?"

"I'll take it." Lolly smiled at Roxie. "That's all a little whore like her is good for anyway."

Lolly sat down on the chair by the dressing table and, leaning back, she slowly raised her skirt to reveal a pair of black lace panties. Sliding them down, Lolly spread her legs; all the while gazing dreamily at Ashley through half-closed eyes.

"Well?" said Roxie to Ashley, who was standing rigidly beside her. "Get down to work then."

Ashley shook her head.

"No."

"*No?*" Enraged, Roxie gripped Ashley by the shoulders and tried to force her to her knees.

"I said *no!*" screamed Ashley. Wrenching away from Roxie, she ran at the door; just as it opened and Pete, Ricky and Marky swaggered in.

Pete and Ricky seized hold of Ashley and moved her back into the middle of the room.

Marky walked over to her. "You know, Ashley… I think I speak for all of us when I say I'm a bit unimpressed with your lack of gratitude. You begged to be on the show — we brought you here! You claimed to be a fan yet all you've done is cry and complain since you got here. And then stabbing poor Roxie in the arm…"

Roxie gave an injured sniffle.

"Now," he said. "We *were* going to bring you onstage for the big finale…"

There was suddenly a rush of voices and pounding feet outside in the corridor.

"*Fuck,*" yelled Roxie. "Little bitch called the cops!"

Ignoring her, Marky continued — addressing Ashley in a gentle, almost paternal manner. "But I think it's best we end this *now*. As a favour from me to you, I'll make it quick."

Grabbing Ashley by the hair, Pete jerked her head back at an angle that exposed her throbbing jugular.

"For fuck's sake, Mark," Lolly urged. "Just do it!"

Marky had the blade raised up when the door crashed open.

"Drop the weapon, son," said the SWAT officer. "That's right. Nice and easy."

There was a second's pause, and Marky dropped the knife to the floor.

21.

"BREAKING NEWS: The names of the three victims recovered from the scene of what has now been dubbed 'The Gigglers Massacre' have been identified as 19-year-old Carla Barrie, 22-year-old William Anderson, and 21-year-old Harold Ferrier."

✄

"FORMER CHILD STARS ARRESTED AT SCENE OF CARNAGE: Roxanne Dennis, Peter Luderer, Mark Rodriguez, Lauren DeWitt & Richard Kilpatrick."

✄

"THE FACES OF EVIL:

What turned these fresh-faced young starlets into KILLERS?"

✄

"SOLE SURVIVOR OF GIGGLER BLOODBATH: 18-year-old Ashley Turner has so far remained silent about her trauma at the hands of the former child stars. Her father, British expatriate, James Turner, has released this statement: 'Our daughter

Ashley has been through a terrible ordeal, and while we are indeed grateful for all the support we've received, we ask that we are given the time and privacy we need to heal as a family.' "

⋈

Ashley was sat in the makeup chair, mentally preparing for her appearance on the Jenny Jenkins Show. They had offered to take her to the studio's greenroom, but Ashley had politely declined.

She hadn't even wanted to appear on the show, but her parents and Dr. Hodges thought, with the anniversary coming up, that telling her story on national television might give her some closure. Closure.

For weeks after the horror, Ashley had been plagued by a recurring nightmare — it was always the same one. She would go to sleep next to her mum, and then, in the dream, Ashley would 'wake up' on the couch back in the Greenroom to see Ricky and Polka-Dot Pete standing over her.

"Ashley. Come on, honey… It's your turn now."

She would wake up screaming then, and it would

sometimes take up to an hour of comforting and reassurance before Ashley was able to fall back to sleep.

Aside from disrupted sleep, she'd also been struggling to eat. No matter how many delicious meals her mother prepared, anything Ashley attempted to eat, she would promptly bring back up. She had been existing solely on soup and had lost over twenty pounds in weight.

Ultimately, it was Ashley's Aunt Nancy who came to the rescue. Jo Ann Hodges — a woman she had trained with at Columbia University, was now practising at a small psychiatric clinic, specialising in post-traumatic stress disorder and bereavement counselling. After a brief discussion with Ashley and her parents, Nancy rang the clinic to arrange a consultation.

Jo Hodges had been a godsend. A striking woman in an olive-green boiler suit, who looked like a female blend of Jimi Hendrix and Freddie Mercury; she and Ashley had clicked immediately over their love of cats. During their first appointment, Ashley had shared with Dr. Hodges a little video she had taken of Jemima on her phone, and then Dr. Hodges had shown Ashley

pictures of Mitchell — her enormous fluffy Maine Coon.

Gradually, Ashley found herself opening up to Dr. Hodges in a way that she had so far felt unable to do with her parents. They spent hours going through the assault in detail and Ashley's feelings of shame and dirtiness attached to it; and later, about the excruciating forensic gynaecological exam carried out to determine the extent of Ashley's injuries. They also talked about Carla, their friendship, and the guilt and anguish Ashley felt over her death.

In conjunction with the therapy sessions, and the medication Dr. Hodges had prescribed to help her sleep, Ashley slowly began to come to terms with her trauma, and, with the support of her family and Jo Hodges, she was able to stand trial against The Gigglers later that year. To spare Ashley the ordeal of facing them in court, she was able to pre-record her statement and undergo cross-examination via video link, away from the intimidating atmosphere of the courtroom.

Then, in September, she had been contacted by the Jenny Jenkins Show. Ashley's first reaction had been to turn the invitation down, as to go on the show would feel like she was exploiting not only *her* experiences, but also the murders of Carla, Will and Harry; but, as Dr. Hodges had pointed out, this could be a chance to pay tribute to their memory, and also to promote the A.S.H.L.E.Y Foundation — a charity she had helped set up to support fellow survivors of similar crimes.

><

Ashley was now sitting on a couch in the glossy television studio telling her story to Jenny Jenkins — a buxom blonde with Tipp-Ex-white teeth and thickly drawn-on eyebrows.

"Well," Ashley continued reluctantly. "Polka-Dot Pete… I mean Peter Luderer… yanked my head back, and Mark — I mean *Marky-Mark*, held the knife up, ready to slit my throat, and then I could have sworn that I had passed on to the other side and was just dreaming… but apparently the SWAT team burst in — just in time…"

Ashley paused, but Jenny's gaze urged her to continue.

"I... I don't know why I survived at all."

"Wow," said Jenny. "Well, Ashley. It's been almost a year, and you've refused to speak to the press — until now? Everyone wants to know — why the silence? And what made you change your mind?"

"Well..." Ashley said. "I haven't wanted to... exploit the situation... It was a horrible thing that happened to me. To all of us."

"Ashley." Jenny chuckled. "What happened to you is *very* different than what happened to those Gigglers. I think I can speak for all of us when I say so." She turned to her studio audience, gesturing them to whoop in agreement.

Ashley smiled nervously.

"Well," Jenny said. "It sounds like you've got a *lot* of support here. Now. You've written a book about your experience. Is that right?"

"Yes," said Ashley.

"Congratulations!" Jenny said. "And thank you

for your courage in sharing your story." She turned and spoke directly to the camera. "And now before the break, we would like to talk to you about the A.S.H.L.E.Y Foundation. Assisting Surviving Hostages to Lead Extraordinary... Yives?"

Confused, Jenny looked to Ashley, who was mouthing something at her.

"Lives!" said Jenny, composed again. "Assisting Surviving Hostages to Lead Extraordinary Lives. A wonderful cause."

⋈

Outside the studio, Ashley was walking to the car. Cameras were flashing and journalists were clamouring for her attention. Ashley had a peacoat on over her taping outfit and she was attempting to shield herself with her coat, her hand, and her notebook.

"Ashley Mary Turner!" one reporter yelled out, making Ashley instinctively turn around. Facing the lenses dead-on, she began to take in the gaggle of flashbulbs, the slew of people all calling her name, all there for *her*.

Ashley's posture straightened from one of penance and persecution, to one of confidence, pride. Beyond pride. A little smile crept onto her face, and she let her peacoat fall softly from her shoulders — Ashley even found herself beginning to vogue a bit, basking in their warmth.

As she turned to leave, Ashley cast one last lingering, flirtatious look towards the cameras.

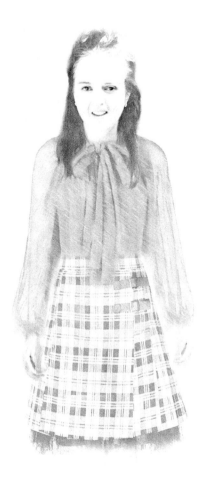

KATY CHARLOTTE GRUBB

AUTHOR'S NOTE

The character of Ashley's psychiatrist is named in memory of my beloved friend and mentor, Jo Ann Hodges, who passed away on the 25th of July, 2017.

Jo helped me overcome my past traumatic experiences in the same way Dr. Hodges helps Ashley in the story. Not a day goes by when I don't think of her, and she will live on in my heart forever.

Jo Ann Hodges

5th June, 1959 – 25th July, 2017

Until we meet again,

Katy xx

Printed in Great Britain
by Amazon

36646938R00108